C000261135

G R JORDAN

The Pirate Club

A Highlands and Islands Detective Thriller

First published by Carpetless Publishing 2020

Copyright © 2020 by G R Jordan

All rights reserved. No part of this publication may be reproduced, stored or transmitted in any form or by any means, electronic, mechanical, photocopying, recording, scanning, or otherwise without written permission from the publisher. It is illegal to copy this book, post it to a website, or distribute it by any other means without permission.

This novel is entirely a work of fiction. The names, characters and incidents portrayed in it are the work of the author's imagination. Any resemblance to actual persons, living or dead, events or localities is entirely coincidental.

G R Jordan asserts the moral right to be identified as the author of this work.

G R Jordan has no responsibility for the persistence or accuracy of URLs for external or third-party Internet Websites referred to in this publication and does not guarantee that any content on such Websites is, or will remain, accurate or appropriate.

Designations used by companies to distinguish their products are often claimed as trademarks. All brand names and product names used in this book and on its cover are trade names, service marks, trademarks and registered trademarks of their respective owners. The publishers and the book are not associated with any product or vendor mentioned in this book. None of the companies referenced within the book have endorsed the book.

First edition

ISBN: 978-1-912153-91-6

This book was professionally typeset on Reedsy.
Find out more at reedsy.com

Contents

Foreword

This story is set in the idyllic yet sometimes harsh landscape of the Hebridean Islands, located in the north-western part of Scotland. Although set amongst known towns and villages, note that all persons and specific places are fictional and not to be confused with actual buildings and structures that exist and which have been used as an inspirational canvas on which to tell a completely fictional story.

Acknowledgement

To Susan, Harold, Evelyn, Pete, Joan, Jean and Rosemary for your work in bringing this novel to completion, your time and effort is deeply appreciated.

Epigraph

Now and then we had a hope that if we lived and were good,
God would permit us to be pirates.

Mark Twain

Chapter 1

The tide lapped on the beach, giving a moment's shimmer to the wet sand before the water sank through the grains and was then replaced by a second wave of froth. Her feet began to sink into the thick gloopy surface, and she felt the chill coming up her leg. Damn, this was good. There was no one on the beach and thankfully the weather had abated from last night allowing her to enjoy this time away from her domineering mother.

How am I hanging with my mother when I'm forty-five years old? The question sat before her as she watched a seagull lift before the tide splashed its feet. *If only I could be as free as it is,* she thought, *if only I could cut the strings and fly.* But with her mother's weak chest, she knew that was not going to happen. And when her mother wanted to come to Barra to chase old dreams from her earlier days, she could not let the woman follow that path alone. Instead, she, Karen, must take her moments as they came, and last night's was breathless.

The fisherman had eyed her up from across the hotel bar. At first, Karen had not even thought about it, but the man was incessant. If she had been wearing something stylish, hell, maybe even something sexy, she might not have been so surprised, but instead she had been in her floppy jumper and long skirt. Mother had been wittering beside her as he looked on from across the room and was oblivious to the eyes she and her mystery man were flashing at each other. Casting a roving eye over his worn but strong body, Karen's mind had drifted off from her mother's talk of prescriptions and doctors and had instead drifted to a beach like this.

When her mother's drink had become empty, she had taken the chance to step up to the bar, ordering from right beside him. As he took in her full figure, she had tried to stand a little provocatively and thought she had failed when her hair came untied at the rear and fell across her face. But he had pushed it back with a gentle hand. When he tried to speak, she had put up a quick hand which sent a sad expression across his face. But she had written him a note on a bar napkin and left it in front of him. 'Eleven o'clock right here,' it had said.

She'd barely hoped he would stay but after mother was safely tucked into bed and Karen had used the excuse of cramping legs and the need for a walk, she had escaped. But not before she had changed into her racy underwear and special top. It was a little more daring and revealed more cleavage than her mother would have contemplated suitable from a 'decent' young woman. Young, as if! It had been six years of looking after her and in that time, Karen had enjoyed one kiss. And it had not been a passionate one, instead delivered by George from accounts at a bus stop on a cold Monday evening. In truth, he was wetter than the weather had been.

Her fisherman had taken her outside into his car, leaving Castlebay, the main settlement on Barra, and had driven over the causeway to Vatersay, the small island with its perfect beaches, just like this one at Traigh Siar. She loved the Gaelic names; it gave it all a little more mystery. But there had been no mystery to his intentions. Not that he was anything but a gentleman. They had exited the car and walked along the beach before he stopped and made his move. Abandoning herself to him, she allowed him to enjoy her as she revelled in her first encounter of a worthy nature in so long. It had been two in the morning when she had sneaked back into the shared room, her mother snoring loudly.

Karen had not slept and so returned to this scene of triumph, listening to the roll of the sea coming ashore as it brought back the memory of passion and hunger. She wanted it all again—the mystery, the excitement, and the conquest. Looking up the beach, she wondered if her underwear was still about and laughed. It had cost a fortune and had been held back for such a moment as this but had been disposed of in a flash after a quick glance. Karen shivered remembering the cold air on her skin, the goose bumps that accompanied last night's exertions.

There's someone at the far end of the beach, thought Karen, her eyes bleary but peering as best they could along its length. A thought struck her. Maybe she had exhausted him so much he was still sleeping here. Surely not after the cold of the night. And had there not been rain as well?

Stepping quickly along the sand in her bare feet, her shoes swinging from her hand, she fixated on the figure, hoping her eyes would focus more clearly before she got close and had to make up some daft excuse why she had made a bee line for this total stranger. And then something skipped in her heart and her stomach felt light. The jacket on this figure was the same colour. And it was a male figure, long coat filled by broad shoulders. His shoulders had been strong and would bare the marks of her nails where she had clung to him in their passion.

She ran.

The sun broke through the grey cloud, lifting the day's dim filter and she saw something gleam in the man's back. As she approached, her pace slowed until she began to stumble and became faint. It could not be, this could not happen. He had been hers, had loved her like nothing she had experienced in her last ten years. It was like being back at university and being with her rugby man on that summer night, the man whose name had faded. But this was not to be a one-night stand; she had seen more, seen a way clear from her mother.

Karen fell to her knees and laid her head on the man's back, right beside where the dagger was protruding. She sent an exploratory hand to his face and began to sob heartily as the cold of his skin reinforced the silence of his body. There was no heartbeat, no rise and fall of his chest. Her fisherman was dead.

* * *

The wind blew onto his cheek and a spit of rain made it feel even colder but Daniel cared not. Here he was free, unburdened by whatever society thought. Back in their south coast home, they would have suffered from stares and even the occasional abusive word from some ignorant passer-by who did not understand love. But here there were so few people, no one to bother them. Especially as it was out of season and the campsite had only the pair of them. Yes, it had been cold, but they had made enough heat together and had spent a wrapped-up night in each other's arms. Yes, they managed that back home but not without the fear of discovery.

Watching his secret partner walk past him and across the small causeway towards Sanday, the small island attached to Canna, Daniel enjoyed the view. James was tall and broad, strong in every respect. His dark blue rain jacket was dotted with rivulets of water that descended slowly down until they fell from its hem line. But the rain was refreshing. Everything here was.

Daniel could have stayed in their tent all morning in James' arms, but his partner had insisted on striking out to see the small church on Sanday. Not that it looked like some great relic but because he had thought it would make a great shot. Everywhere James went, his camera went with him and Daniel thought it was the secret lover in their relationship, the one he could not quite budge. But it did not matter, for it took them away from that bloody town and its hateful attitudes.

'Hey,' shouted James, 'stand there on the bridge, just to the side so I can get the background in, the sea sweeping beyond.'

Daniel positioned himself as requested and then accepted James' kiss for his efforts. His tightly curled hair, along with his black skin, was adored by James and he had never felt more appreciated by any other white man. Not that there was any difference between them, they were simply a pair, why could everyone else not see that? His parents, James' parents, the rugby team at the university. But now was not the time for these thoughts.

'Can you get down to the beach over the side of the causeway. I know it's rocky, but it will look great. Give me a minute when you get there, just going to change a filter. The sun's playing havoc with the lighting.'

Daniel clambered down to the shore at the far side of the

causeway, struggling with his small backpack that contained their drinks and snacks for this trip. Setting it down behind him, he looked into the tiny crevices between the sharp stone and sought the myriad of creatures whose lives existed wholly in these forgotten cracks of the world. *I wish I could simply fall into one of these cracks*, he thought, *away from anyone, away from prying eyes. But then again, I'm prying, am I not? Someone will always want to look and comment.*

'There's something behind you, Danny, right on the shore, just beyond the rocks there. It's in the shot, can you move it?'

Daniel nodded and spun around looking for the offending item. Being further away, James had obviously failed to see it was a boot and Daniel decided he should simply grab it and throw it. It was a proper hiking boot too, real expensive but would be useless as a single. As he got closer, he could see another boot just beside it and his heart rose as he wondered if the size would be right.

Then Daniel saw the leg. 'James, there's someone here.'

'Stop being bloody paranoid and just get it out of shot.'

'James, there's someone in the boots, I can see legs.'

'What the hell are you talking about, Danny? I have the shot all lined up so just get the item shifted. Quick, the light will change again.'

Reluctantly, Daniel continued towards the boots, his eyes trying to look with just the peripheral of his vision. He could see a pair of white legs and then a skirt that was billowed up to just below the woman's bottom. Yes, the legs were too slender for a man. 'James, come here, now! There's a person here—she might be in trouble.'

'Every flaming time I get a shot you get spooked by something. There's no bastard here, Danny. That's why we came, that's what you wanted. You and me, alone, and you still make up people coming to look at you. You still go on and on about the . . .'

James stood with an open mouth looking at the white legs. Stepping forward, he followed them up to the skirt and then to the rain jacket that covered the body. It was yellow but it seemed to have some sort of stain on it.

'What the hell, Danny? Is she all right? Touch her—see if she's breathing.'

'I'm not. You don't touch the dead; just leave them, just leave it.'

'She might be in trouble, Danny. Look, I'll get her.' James stepped forward and placed a large hand on the woman's shoulder. She could only be about five-foot-tall, and her blonde hair looked matted and stained as well. With a quick yank, James twisted her body over. As he did the head began to turn but then fell further backwards revealing a cut that had severed through the throat, causing the head to almost flop off completely.

Turning away, James vomited onto the rocks behind him. Daniel stumbled backwards until his feet caught on rocks and he fell backwards landing inches deep in the receding tide. 'James! James. Holy God, James. She's dead, she's dead!' But James was still on his knees, emptying whatever was left in his stomach, his eyes full of tears.

Chapter 2

'Hope! Hope! Are you still in that shower?'

Hope remained bent double with the water splashing her neck before running down and then either working its way across her sheltered front or dropping down to the floor. She felt so tired. But things had been so busy, what with the Sergeant's exam and then the promotion. The shower room door was flung open.

'Hope, it's work. Sounds bad. I think you need to get ready.' She heard Allinson's voice and wanted to stand up straight and smile at her man, but she felt lethargic. But it would pass, it always did. 'Are you all right?'

'Fine,' said Hope. 'Just tired.' With that she brought herself up to her full height and gingerly stepped out of the shower. The lethargy had suddenly passed but her muscles were still somewhat tight, causing her to wince a little.

'You're not okay, are you?' Allinson insisted, dropping a towel around her and then wrapping his arms around her, too.

'Stop fussing. What did they say was up?'

'Double murder, apparently. One in Canna and the other in Barra. Macleod wants you in quick and said to pack a bag. I guess our dinner's off tonight.'

Hope smiled as she leaned back to whisper in Allinson's ear,

'You've seen plenty of me this last week. I could do with the sleep.'

'You didn't complain. Anyway, time for the Sergeant to go to work.'

The title resonated with Hope, something inside giving her a mix of pride and power. She liked her colleagues, DCs Ross and Stewart, Ross being the calm and polite gent, and Kirsten with her glasses forever being pushed up high onto that nose. But although she acted like the senior before, now she had the rank and was confirmed the superior officer. She would see the change in Macleod too, his pride in her promotion, feeling like a real unit now, all the correct staff in place. When she was still a constable, he had stuck with her when he could have asked for a sergeant.

'Right, you need to let go and let me get dried,' she told Allinson and he let his hands fall away. As he reached the door, he turned and simply stood watching her. With the satisfaction of a strutting peacock, she dried herself, basking in his joy at her before wrapping the towel around herself and pushing him out of the door. Fifteen minutes later, Hope was standing with a bag and letting Allinson hold her head to his chest, his fingers ruffling the red hair he had removed from its ponytail.

'Enough!'

'Never,' he said.

'I need to go,' and Hope broke off and tied her hair back up behind her head. 'I'll ring tonight, wherever I am. We never get a moment, do we?' This was true in one sense in that every liaison this week had been after ten o'clock at night with work completed. Allinson had faithfully come round to her house and waited for her. He had cooked and massaged and generally been everything she had wanted from him and she had been his willing lover in return. But the experience on holiday, when he had complained about her lack of clothing when sunbathing had changed the relationship. Yes, they had made up afterwards, but they had not resolved it. What would happen next time? In the meantime, they carried on regardless.

As Hope drove into the car park of the Inverness police station, she saw her boss, DI Macleod, stepping out of his car with a worried look on his face. He was not one for smiling in excess and in some ways his familiar visage was a comfort. As she got out of her car, she saw he had waited by the rear entrance to the station.

'Sergeant! Well done, Hope. I was going to have a little celebration, but we need to move. My office in five minutes.'

And with that he was gone. Taking her bag from the boot of the car, Hope quickly went to her locker and then made a beeline for Macleod's office. The door was open, and Macleod was behind his desk sipping a coffee as she walked in. Standing before the large solid fixture were Ross and Stewart. Ross turned to her as she walked in and offered a hand which she shook.

'Boss, well done.'

'No, Ross, never boss. I'll accept Sarge, but the boss is behind that desk—isn't that right, sir?'

Macleod looked up from his coffee. 'And never forget it,' he said with a smile. Macleod seemed to be waiting for Stewart to say her piece to Hope but the woman just nodded and gently slid the thick-rimmed glasses onto her nose once more. Kirsten Stewart, the newest member of the team after impressing on the Isle of Lewis was making her mark in many ways. Macleod seemed fascinated in the way the woman thought things through, and she had bonded with Ross almost seamlessly.

'What's the news, sir?' asked Hope.

'A body found on Vatersay off Barra. Stabbed on the beach, found by a woman he had picked up at a bar the previous night. That's where myself and Stewart are going. You and Ross will be heading to Canna where a woman's almost decapitated body was found by the shore. Although it was in the water, it was a recent kill, a large knife wound that almost took off the head, or at least that's the initial thoughts but you'll need a forensics team to confirm that.'

'Have I got Mackintosh?' asked Hope. Mackintosh was the senior forensics investigator in the area and was also extremely fond of Macleod. And she was not afraid to show it.

'No, she's going to Barra. We need to fly to Glasgow and then up to Barra. And don't give me those eyes, Sergeant. Mackintosh made the decision; they are her people. I just need teams out and about from her; I don't deploy her people.'

'Of course,' said Hope but noticed Stewart fiddling with her glasses.

'The local coastguard has sealed off your scene, but they are going to need help, so we have sent some officers over via Mallaig. But it's your case, Sergeant, just keep me informed. Ross has more detail, but you can read that on the way. So, a fair bit of travelling, everyone, and given the locations I say we are going to be fairly stretched, so keep in touch. Dismissed. I'll see you outside, Stewart,' said Macleod and then held up his hand to Hope.

'Yes, sir,' she said once the others had left.

'You know how to do this, Hope. You might be nervous as I'm letting you run the job totally but remember if I didn't think you could do this, you wouldn't be here. And you have me on the end of a phone. Don't be afraid to call.'

'Yes, sir. Thanks for the vote of confidence. Good luck at your end.'

'Oh, and Hope, how's things at home with Allinson?'

'None of your business, sir. But better.'

'Only better?' asked Macleod.

'As I said none of your business.' She smiled but Hope knew he could see the cracks in the relationship.

'Okay,' said a resigned Macleod, 'catch me a killer.'

Vatersay was connected to the Isle of Barra by a single causeway and Macleod thought the place similar to Lewis, his place of birth. Wild to a large degree with houses hewn into the uneven terrain, there was also a sense of community in the few townships that were across the island. But the most striking feature was the sea air that filled his lungs. Yes, Inverness was by the coast, but this was the west side of Scotland, altogether more bracing, as you looked out towards the Atlantic with the wind blowing through your hair.

Their cases had been dropped at the local hotel and as the car pulled up beside Traigh Shiar, Macleod could see only green broken by rocky outcrops. The beach itself was hidden from the single-track road and as he looked for the sea in that direction, he could only see sky as the land rose slightly before presumably falling down to the beach.

There were a number of cars present, one a marked police car, and Macleod saw a number of locals standing around, surveying all that was happening. Hazel Mackintosh, the forensics lead who had travelled with them, took a bag from the car and made her way towards the beach, quickly followed by Macleod who feared she would quarantine the area before he got there.

Passing underneath a single overhead wire, Macleod heard what sounded like an angry teacher as Mackintosh disappeared down to the sand.

'Has that body been moved? Tell me, Sergeant, have you moved that body? There's no way that body is where you found it. Look it's been dragged, clumsily too.'

As Macleod cleared the small rise of ground, he saw Mackintosh stabbing a finger into a uniformed Sergeant who looked like he was facing the hell of his nightmares. There was another uniformed officer standing close by, but he did not seem to want to come to the aid of his sergeant.

Stewart approached Macleod from behind and took in the scene before pushing her glasses up to her nose and murmuring in a low voice to Macleod, 'They had to move the body because of the tide, Sir. Might have gone to sea.'

Of course, Stewart was right, and Macleod walked quickly over to the angry Mackintosh. 'Mackintosh, a word, please.'

'A word? You can have a word with these island clowns, wrecking my crime scene.'

'Mackintosh, a word, over here,' said Macleod, indicating they should step away to a discreet area. When she did not move, Macleod took her arm and wheeled her away.

'What the hell are you doing?' thundered Mackintosh.

'Listen,' said Macleod in a whisper.

'Don't listen me . . .'

'Listen! Hazel, please listen. They moved the body because the tide would have swept it away. Hopefully, they have photographs, and if they don't by all means continue to give them the rounds of the houses. However, we are a long way from home, and we need all the help we can get so let's be a little more professional and demur when it comes to our colleagues. And they have an audience. They don't have many officers here and they don't need you making out they are incompetent to the general population. Understood?'

The woman's eyes were all fire, but Macleod could see the brain ticking and realising his point. Hazel Mackintosh was a full-on charging rhino and got things done but here on the edge you maybe needed a little more tact.

'I'll make it right, Seoras. Thank you.'

'It's okay, just tread lightly, Hazel.' And then he realised he had used her first name. The woman smiled before turning away and he knew he had been lured in by her show of vulnerability. The trouble with Hazel Mackintosh for Macleod was that she wanted him, she had made that much clear, but she had also not been so crass or rude as to make a direct approach for a man with a partner. Instead she lulled him into little conceits, such as using her first name in a professional capacity. Only Hope had earned that privilege, having been there for him. But even then, not in front of others.

'Stewart,' shouted Macleod and pointed to the Sergeant so recently berated. It was time to get a proper debrief on what had happened and not a simple report. And besides, he needed to mend a few bridges after that prominent display by Hazel. And there it was again. She's Mackintosh, always Mackintosh. As if on cue, his eyes caught the sight of Mackintosh looking back and she gave him a cheeky smile, like the escaping captain of a pirate vessel letting the king's own navy know that they have been licked.

'Sergeant, I'm DI Macleod and this is DC Stewart. I read the report you sent over. Have you any more detail on the victim or who he may have been with?'

'Sergeant McNeil, sir. You are looking at one of Scotland's

finest singers but maybe only known in the Gaelic world. He was a former Mod singer, a gold medal winner too but that was maybe thirty years ago. Today he was little washed up. His name is Alasdair MacPhail.'

'A local?' asked Stewart.

'No, he resides on Harris according to the last address we have for him but he's originally from Skye. He spent last night wooing a female on holiday with her mother, a Miss Karen Barton, from Coventry, who had sex with the man right on this beach before returning to her hotel. A right illicit affair, what with her sneaking out from her mother in the middle of the night.' The Sergeant shook his head and scanned the length of the beach as if looking of the site of last night's liaisons.

'A young woman?' asked Macleod.

'Oh, no. Well, not a kid. She's,' the Sergeant flicked through his notebook, 'forty-five.'

'And she's disappearing secretly from her mother?'

'Not sure she's doing this sort of thing on a regular basis, sir. There's CCTV at the hotel that confirms her timings for her movements. And she says she had not met Mr MacPhail before last evening. She reckoned he was a fisherman and when he checked her out at the bar, her words not mine, she just took a chance. She has no record for anything, not even a parking ticket.'

'Well, I 'd like to see her,' said Macleod, 'do you have the name of the hotel?'

'Of course, sir, and we can take you there directly. We have a hire car for you at the hotel and your office said you'd want a hall or space to work. We have commandeered a recreational hall in Castlebay for your team. Just ask if you need something but bear in mind, we are a little further out here so it may take time for certain requests.'

'It's been a while since you had a murder here on Barra?' asked Stewart.

'You could say that,' the sergeant replied, 'not within my lifetime anyway. In truth, it's spooking out the local community, so I warn you to take it carefully with them.'

'I understand, Sergeant—at least it was not a local man; then you really would see fear and maybe panic. And with an English lady being involved I guess she might get the blame amongst the local networks.'

The Sergeant tilted his head to one side almost apologetically and pointed to an officer who was standing at the edge of the beach. 'That's James, over here from Glasgow. He'll sort you out when you want to leave here, sir.'

'Very good,' said Macleod. 'I'll take a look at the body and then we'll interview our witness.'

'Oh, if you do, sir, I'd take care. Don't do it with the mother around. She's something of a grumpy cow.'

'I'm sure you mean she's an obstinate or interfering woman, sergeant. Thanks for your help.' The man's face dropped as Macleod turned away and a push of the glasses from Stewart reinforced the point.

Macleod realised that Mackintosh was putting on her white coverall and was temporarily away from the body, so he quietly walked up as close as he could. There were a number of footprints and he could see where the body had been dragged until the markings stopped at what he presumed would have been where the tide last reached. Taking an acute angle, he walked closer placing his feet where there were no footprints.

The man was hunched over on the sand with the knife sticking out of his back and placed in up to the hilt. The knife was ornate, with a black handle and some gemstones. Whether they were expensive or not, Macleod had no idea.

'Why leave that knife in his back, sir?'

'Time, being seen, or worried that they had?' mused Macleod.

'No, sir, it makes no sense unless they wanted to leave a note to others. There's a risk of fingerprints or material. From here it looks like he was stabbed more than once too. Seems a bit strange to me.'

'Noted, Stewart, but we'll leave the actual analysis of the method to Mackintosh.'

Macleod knelt and examined the body from a distance for another two minutes during which time Stewart left to walk along the beach. As he looked at the man's face, he heard someone walk up behind him and then kneel beside him. He smelt the perfume and recognised the figure as Mackintosh even though she was just behind him.

'Let me know how you get on,' said Macleod. 'I take it the team are here on the ferry as soon as.'

'Yes, another hour maybe. But I'll get started and have something for you shortly. From a distance it looks like that jacket was punctured more than once. And those positions say it was done by someone with the knowledge of which organs to hit. It looks like a proper take down, Seoras, not a random act.'

'Unlikely to be a frenzy then, say from an embarrassed or scorned lover?'

'No, Seoras, not at all.'

'Well let me know what else you turn up.'

'Seoras, what time shall I tell the hotel for dinner tonight?' Macleod flashed a worried look. 'I mean for all of us,' said

Mackintosh.

'I wouldn't book anything as I don't know when we'll be finished but thanks for thinking of it, Hazel.' He had said it again. And she was smiling about it. Macleod shook his head clear and walked back to the green grass that was cut through the middle by the single-track road. *Time to see our witness.*

Chapter 3

The boat taking them across to Canna was a motor vessel and capable of holding around twelve people by Hope's calculations. With the extra police officers and the forensic team, it was almost full, and she felt a little crowded and chose to sit at the rear of the boat on an outside piece of deck to get some air. Things moved so fast in this job. *One minute I was happily enjoying the company of my man and the next we are likely to be apart for who knows how long.* At least Allinson understood; he was a police officer, too.

Sometimes she wondered if she had dented his career by becoming attached to him. He had slid sideways to join another department and he was still a constable while she had climbed to Sergeant. But that was his fault, as he had concentrated on things outside of work. His band for instance, that he quietly disappeared off to, but then raised merry hell with in some random pub around the north of Scotland. Yes, she enjoyed watching him throw those drumsticks down onto the skins of the kit, but it got in the way of his promotion. She was three years behind him in terms of time in the force but already she was a rank above.

Ross sat down beside her and took out some of the case notes to go over. *Everything was sketchy at this time*, thought Hope, *but once we get to the scene, that should be cleared up.* Canna was one of the Small Isles, just south of Skye and was only four miles square. With a population of less than thirty, it was more of a place people visited rather than lived in, but a small band were trying to change that. Hope had also been advised that her mobile would not work although the island did have broadband and telephone access.

The sea spray kept her face chilled as she crossed over, but she preferred that to the claustrophobic conditions inside the main cabin. Looking around her, she saw faces occasionally glancing at her, knowing she was the boss today but not sure of who she was. Having Ross beside her was a comfort and the man was acting as normal, in his calm and methodical approach to policing.

'When we get there, Ross, we get forensics to the scene and secure it fully. Then we grab our witnesses, after which we go round the islanders and see if anyone noticed anything untoward. I guess it's important to establish who this is but also were they killed on Canna or did the body float there? And if Canna, why there? If this is a local issue, then that scares me frankly, a murderer running round such a small area with thirty people there for the taking. And no police presence once we exhaust what we can do.'

Ross nodded and then pointed towards a small harbour that was approaching fast. There were no other vessels there and Hope wondered how often the ferry ran to this place. A lack of vehicles was going to be an issue, but she had been assured that the local population would help, shocked as they were by this tragic death.

Stepping off the boat, Hope was met by a man in the distinctive blue of the coastguard and shook his hand.

'Andrew Farmer, Station Officer Canna Coastguard. Welcome, Detective, but forgive me if I say we are not glad to see you. Terrible business. But we have kept it as best we can until your arrival. There's a minibus here but I might need two trips as there's a good few of you. This way please.'

He never even asked my name, thought Hope, *never wanted to know who was in charge*. In her head she saw Macleod step after the man and take him by the shoulder to let him know who the boss was. Well if it was good enough for Macleod. Hope strode quickly and tapped Andrew farmer on the shoulder.

'Detective Sergeant Hope McGrath, Mr Farmer. I'll be leading the team while here, but you can direct any queries to either myself or DC Ross, who is the rather tall and dapper man at the rear. We'll need some transport later to go door to door and interview the island. There's not many of you here, I take it.'

'We're all here,' snapped the man. 'This is where we make our lives; it's not a holiday home.'

Hope sighed under her breath; she had not meant it that way. 'I meant that no one was away on business, sir, or had left the island since this happened.'

'No, no one has. In truth we are all a little shocked, so I think the sooner we get this cleared up the better. I reckon she might have floated in, but she hasn't been in the water awfully long. Maybe dumped off a boat.'

'Why do you say that?'

'Well, she was wet through but there's not much change in the skin. They change, get bloated and that, go very white if they have been in the water a long time.' Hope nodded; she was well aware of these sorts of occurrences. 'But this woman had none of that. Of course, we did not go any closer than we had to. Except we did move her slightly in case the tide took her away.'

'Did you photograph her before moving?'

'Yes, we did ask the station up in Stornoway and they said they talked to your people who said it was okay to keep the body safe. And yes, they did ask for lots of photographs. The station will have them if your guys don't. We sent them all.'

Hope climbed into the front seat of the minibus and watched Mr Farmer count all the forensic team in and a single uniformed officer. 'Ross, stay here and get the other officers on a door to door. I'll see you down at the scene when you have these guys going. I hope it doesn't rain.'

The weather was drab, a grey curtain hanging over everything but so far it had not rained, yet the darkness of the clouds gave credence to the general belief that may happen later. They set off in the minibus and Hope watched the small gravelly road disappear behind her as they wound their way beside a low stone wall. The crime scene was a mere kilometre as the crow flies, but it took slightly longer than anticipated due to the curving nature of their route. But soon Hope could see a wooden bridge, wide enough for vehicles but also surrounded by a small number of blue uniformed volunteers.

Hope watched the forensic team begin to cordon off the scene around the bridge and waited a moment while the coastguard officers departed. Giving each of them a verbal 'thank you', she then approached the senior forensic officer for an initial assessment. Of course, Macleod had taken Mackintosh who they worked with before whereas Hope now had a new officer to deal with, one who had only recently moved to the area.

From behind, Jona Nakamura stood only five-foot-tall with

a shimmering run of black hair that reached half-way down her back, or would have if she had not tied it up and then tucked it away inside her coverall suit. On the ferry over she had seemed aloof, not just from Hope but also from her colleagues. She also seemed noticeably young which was a phrase Hope was not used to. The woman would be at least around twenty-five to get to her position in the forensics team, but she looked like she had barely seen her twenties. *Lucky her,* thought Hope.

'Miss Nakamura,' said Hope, causing the woman to spin round, 'do you have any initial thoughts for me.'

'She's not been dead more than maybe two days at most, probably less. Definitely a struggle given the bruising I can see and killed quite brutally. Someone held her from behind and sliced into her throat. It did not slice cleanly, however, and there was a struggle, but they continued and eventually almost severed the head; the neck is cut almost right through. But it was not a clean cut, more of a sawing action so the assailant would be quite strong in comparison to our victim.'

'Delightful' muttered Hope. 'Any identification?'

'Over here,' said the officer and took Hope down the side of the bridge to where a number of items had been laid out in the grass but all bagged. 'We have a wallet of sorts, more a sporty type than a man's wallet. Inside we found bank cards and a driver's licence. According to these items, the woman is Jane Thorne of an Oban address. I'd place her in her fifties or sixties, Sergeant. That's about all so far but I'll see what more we can find out. Do we have anywhere to set up as a temporary office?'

Oh hell, I forgot to ask Farmer about that. 'We'll be sorted soon,' said Hope smiling and then made a beeline for Andrew Farmer. 'Thanks for your assistance, Mr Farmer; your team can stand down now. Is there somewhere we can get accommodations for the night and maybe a small hall to set our things up in? I doubt we'll be here more than a day or so, but we will need to find some beds.'

'There's a right few of you,' the man replied, 'but I'll see what we can do. You may have to double up. I'm not sure what the guest house has available, but I'll come back to you, Sergeant.'

Hope watched the forensic team continue their work before walking back along the road they had travelled to find Ross spreading out the uniformed officers. The tall man smiled as she approached and looked up at the drizzle that had started to fall.

'When I took up policing, this is the type of day I longed for—a cold, dreich afternoon with a slight wind to try and chill you on an island with no mobile signal and little transport.'

'I actually enjoy the outdoors,' replied Hope. 'Maybe you should let me and John take you camping.'

'I'll go clubbing with you,' he laughed. 'Do you have everything you need?'

'Honestly, Ross, I don't know why but I'm a little off balance, not having Macleod here. I want to see the men who found the body. It's all a bit haphazard here, isn't it? I guess they are at the campsite; the report did say that's where they were staying.'

'Camping in this weather, they must be mad.'

'Depends on who's keeping you warm, Ross. Look, Farmer's going to get us set up with a hall and somewhere to stay, so get the island covered, statements and the usual and I'll see our happy tourists. Then we'll reconvene inside wherever Farmer gets us and sort out what we know. I'll need to update Macleod then as well.'

Twenty minutes later, Hope had found the campsite just as the rain began to fall more heavily and looked at the single tent in the field. For two people it was reasonably generous which Hope was thankful for. This would be her first tent interview and the thought of lying down to grill someone about what they had seen was laughable.

Approaching the tent, Hope rapped the side and shouted a hello. The front door was unzipped and the face of a black man, young but worried, looked at her.

'DS McGrath, from Inverness. I'm here to see Daniel and James—is that you?' The man nodded. 'Can I come in?'

Without a word, the tent door was fully opened, and Hope stepped inside and almost immediately had to kneel down to avoid touching the sides of the tent. Inside the place was a mess with upturned sleeping bags and cooking items and clothes scattered about.

'Sorry that your holiday has been ruined,' said Hope. 'Seeing things like that tends to cause the strongest to feel their worst. Can I ask why you are here, on Canna?'

'Just a holiday,' said the white man who was sitting at the rear of the tent. 'I'm James, James Talon and that's Daniel, Danny if you want, Danny Adebayo. We're both from Plymouth, at college there.'

'Flatmates?' asked Hope.

'Friends,' said James.

'Lovers,' interrupted Daniel in a sullen tone. Eyes flashed across the tent and Hope could feel the awkwardness of the situation.

'So why here?'

'It's not easy back at the college. You think it would for two men to be together but with our skin colours we can't really

25

act as we would want back there.'

'Really,' said Hope quite surprised. 'We get some homophobia and race issues up here, but I thought down south would be more tolerant. How long have you been here?'

'Three days,' said James,' We were just out walking when we saw the body by the bridge, and well, it was not pleasant.'

'I was posing for James, he likes to take photographs of me,' said Daniel. 'We can't really do that easily back home, not slightly riskier ones anyway. Lots of space around here away from people. No one to offend and at night no one cares.'

'Did you recognise the victim?' asked Hope.

'No, why would we?'

'Have you noticed anyone out of place here? Anyone who does not seem to be from the island?'

'Hard to tell having only got here but I don't think we have seen anyone except the site owner and maybe two other locals until we found the body. They gave us some whiskey and that, but since then, we have stayed here really. We thought the place would be swarming and we didn't want any attention.'

Hope tried to shuffle as her legs were starting to go to sleep but when the tent sides began to shake, she stopped and saw James' horrified eyes. 'Give me contact details, and also your schedule for the next weeks. I'll be discreet, gentlemen, but I will need to see the photographs you have in your camera. It's to see if you have caught anyone in the background. I take it there's nothing too saucy in there.'

'No,' said James, 'I'm a proper photographer, not some guy collecting porn images. It's all Danny in them but he's not undressed or anything.'

'Too risky, that sort of thing, Officer,' said Danny, almost wistfully.

That night Hope stood in the makeshift hall looking around at the laptops and other technical gear the team had brought over with them. The space was cramped, really tight, but had been bustling that evening. The woman had come over only on the day of the murder and had been spotted by several locals, along with two boats who had moored in the harbour. Despite checking AIS records, the Automatic Identification System that sent out a signal, no boats could be identified and no persons from the boats could be described in any fashion by the local population.

But the real find of the day was brought to Hope by Jona Nakamura and had been discovered in a secret compartment on the victim's coat. It was a scrap of parchment and had instructions on one side, in a calligraphy script and a map on the reverse. The map seemed to show Canna, but it was in large detail and there were no markings on it. The instructions on the reverse required you to have another piece of map to use places marked to fix a final position. This was done by grid markings on the map that ran along its sides, but they were not from the normal Ordnance survey grid.

It was now midnight and Hope had stared at the map for over an hour thinking about how to proceed. All she had was a map she couldn't use and a name. Tomorrow, she would go to Oban and chase up the address from the woman's identification. A car had visited but there had been no signs of life in the house. Neighbours had said they were out and would return tomorrow though they had not known where they had gone. And it was they. A man and a woman.

Leaving one constable in the hall overnight, Hope trudged through the drizzle and dark to the guest house which had left the door unlocked. Due to numbers, Hope would be sharing a room with Jona Nakamura and she found the woman in her pyjamas on the floor cross-legged and with her eyes closed.

'Sorry, I didn't mean to disturb,' said Hope. 'I'll give you a while longer if you want.'

'It's okay, come in. You look exhausted.' By contrast, the Japanese woman looked almost fresh, her long hair now running down her light green top.

'I thought I might take a shower and then get to bed. Got a lot on my mind with this one. All very bizarre, finding a map like that and little else. Whoever killed her wasn't seen at all.'

'The address was no good?'

'Not so far, but I'll go over there tomorrow. Ah, good,' said Hope looking across the room. 'They gave us the en suite. I'll just use the shower.'

When Hope emerged from the bathroom, she was in her own pyjamas and was glad she had packed a pair. Normally she wore nothing in bed but she carried a spare set just in case the places she stayed at were cold. She hadn't expected to share a room.

'You still look exhausted, Sergeant, if you don't mind me saying.'

'Hey, it's Hope up here. No point with all that formality when we have to share like sisters.' Hope laughed. She'd never had any siblings and she thought it was something she had missed out on having heard Allinson talk about his family.

'Jo then, not Jona. My friends just call me Jo.'

'Do you meditate often?' asked Hope.

'Daily, it's good for you . . . but you need a bit more than meditation. Your shoulders are wound up tight.'

'Yes, well, my man's at home so I'll have to just suffer.'

'Kneel down,' said Jona, 'and just close your eyes.' Hope

wondered what the woman was about to do and felt a little trepidation in case she had missed some sort of feeling in the room. A pair of delicate hands started to rub her shoulders, thumbs slowly working into the aches and strains that were pulling at them.

'Better?'

'Hell, yes, don't stop. And Jo.'

'Yes?'

'Next time we need forensics, forget Mackintosh, okay. You're up, girl. Although I'm not sure Macleod will let you do this.' They laughed. *But he damn well should!*

Chapter 4

Macleod looked at his watch and saw the hour was just past ten. The night had come in some time ago and he had retired to their hotel realising that there was little else to be done tonight. Mackintosh had sat down to eat with him and the rest of the team, but she had been subdued, maybe after his ticking off earlier, or maybe she was simply shattered. It had been a long day and they needed sleep. There had been no identification left on the man's body and so it was a wait for possible DNA matches or dental record checks to give confirmation to the ID on the victim. But the locality made it awkward for things to run as smoothly as they would on the mainland or even on Lewis. Yet the local sergeant was sure the victim was Alasdair MacPhail.

People used to always laugh about his home being on the edges of civilisation and he even remembered the comedy show and the weekly skit showing the Hebridean broadcasting corporation. The actor played a bumbling oaf of a man and he thought it somewhat cruel even back in the day. The islands were normal in a lot of ways, people all with their satellite dishes and internet connections. But there was definitely a wild side to the place, winds that blew hard, power cuts during the storms and a simple remoteness. He felt it more here on

Barra than on Lewis. Or maybe he was just somewhere new, for he had never been on Barra before.

His thoughts turned to Hope, and he reckoned she was doing well from her report just a few moments ago. Now, she really was somewhere remote, but at least she would not have many press after her out on Canna. Most people saw Hope as a strong, confident woman, her confidence highlighting her good looks and the striking red hair but Macleod had seen the other side of her, a place most of us have where the doubts creep in and we blindly ignore the strengths we have for our shameful weaknesses. Their relationship had been difficult for him, but she had helped him enormously and he felt he had been able to reciprocate—a far cry from their starting point.

After making coffee, Macleod grabbed his TV remote and decided to pass away an hour before bed. He didn't care what was on as it would just be background noise while his mind scrambled over the case. When a case was running, he could never truly switch off. With no Jane to help him, it would be worse, and a screen was nothing compared to a cheeky brunette who could ease his tensions or lift him out of self-pity if a case was not proceeding well. But a TV was all he had.

There was a cry from outside his window. Macleod forced himself from his bed and was at the window within seconds as another cry struck the air. Looking down to the road outside, he saw a young man of maybe twenty punching an older man, more akin to Macleod's age, right in the teeth. Blood was spilt and the young man was shouting in the older man's face. Macleod could not make out the words but instead turned on his heel shouting to the air for Stewart as he ran through the hotel. Never a coward and always ready to engage anyone who

31

was causing trouble, Macleod was also well aware that these days his fighting prowess was somewhat lacking compared to the fit young bucks coming up behind him. Hope and Stewart could both mix it having been trained in martial arts whereas Ross was simply a strong and tall individual. There was no shame in calling for assistance.

As Macleod cleared the front door of the hotel and ran around the corner to the roadside where he had seen the commotion, he picked up the shouting from the fight. Someone was demanding where something was and was not getting a response. As the perpetrator came into view, Macleod watched the older man crumble and hurtled towards the younger man.

'Police, stand down now!'

The younger man looked over at the advancing Macleod. 'Aye, right. Did they send you from the retirement home?'

The anger swelled in Macleod, which was never a good thing, and he tore at the man who readied himself for Macleod's attack. Abruptly halting as he reached this younger foe, Macleod tried to grab the man's arm, but the man was fast and sidestepped, delivering a blow to Macleod's ribs. He felt the wind being knocked from him and then fought to get his arms before him as another blow rained towards his head. The fog of his hands did enough to deflect the blows, but he was now back peddling with the younger man advancing.

Macleod stumbled and fell. The man looked around him before picking up a piece of metal pipe from the roadside. Trying to scramble away, Macleod got tangled up in his own feet and watched as the man raised his pipe and readied himself for a vicious blow.

'Stop, police!' It was Stewart's voice.

The man stepped back off Macleod before looking at his

new target. Macleod pushed himself off to the side as Stewart continued.

'Put the pipe down and get on your knees. Now! Pipe down and knees!'

Glancing round, Macleod saw his newest member of the team standing in a black silk dressing gown with bare legs below her midthigh. The gown was tied like a judo outfit and she still wore the trademark glasses, pushing them up as she looked at her opponent.

'Bloody hell, first an old man and now a dumpster!'

Unlike himself, Stewart showed no reaction to the remark which Macleod believed would have hurt. He knew Kirsten was sensitive about her weight, or rather her look. While being small, she was also well-built and he thought of her like a powder keg, compact but explosive. But she was also one of those women whose muscles were not seen to the fore due to the curvy nature of her body, and someone cruel would say it was due to overeating or a lack of exercise. In Stewart's case, it was most definitely genetics.

As she approached, the man made a swing at her head which she stepped back from and then advanced, grabbing him by the arm. But he kept coming and she took a blow to her head which sent her glasses flying. It was like she had not been hit and she drove an elbow into his guts causing him to stumble backwards as she continued to hold his arm. Pulling him back to her, she followed up with a knee to the stomach. The man momentarily reared backwards before driving his shoulder low at her and taking them both to the ground.

'Feisty, big girl,' said the man breathlessly. Macleod tried to rise but he was feeling groggy from the punch and was struggling to co-ordinate to his feet. He watched the man sit up on top of Stewart and fire a punch on her face. She took it on the chin before grabbing his shoulders and driving a knee between his legs. She then threw him off and rolled up to her feet, ready to go again.

The man looked at Stewart and then at Macleod who was now beginning to rise. There were further shouts around the corner making the summation of his situation a negative one, for the man took off along the road into the night. Macleod collapsed back to the ground.

'Sir?' shouted Stewart.

'Him,' said Macleod, pointing to the old man and watched Stewart race to the man. A hand then grabbed Macleod, helping him to his feet, and he looked into the eyes of an older woman, one of the bar staff if he remembered correctly. Everything was just a little unsteady.

A few minutes later, Macleod was sitting in the bar area, slouched in a seat, watching Stewart and one of the staff tending to the wounds on the old man. He had been cut and suffered some blood loss, but he was talking in a perfectly erudite fashion and any immediate alarm was definitely extinguished. When they had finished applying some bandages to the man, Macleod carefully made his way over to him and plonked himself on the seat next to the man. Stewart was kneeling on the floor before him, tending to a wound on the man's hand and Macleod thought she looked different. Yes, she was in a dressing gown and sweating from her battle with the young assailant but there was something else wrong. Her glasses. She had no glasses on.

'Are you up to a few questions, sir?' asked Macleod.

'I think so, sir. Thank you, I was properly getting my backside kicked there, wasn't I? Until you came in, and then

34

this, I hope you don't mind me saying this, my dear angel arrived.'

Macleod watched Stewart's face and swore he detected the hint of a smile. 'Just doing my job, sir. That hand looks fine, but I think you should get to the hospital. I believe they have a small one here,' said Stewart.

'Don't be daft. Had worse than this back in my fighting days. Maggie sent us out there and we did a job, did we not? Survived that and I'll survive this. But your face is a healing balm that no hospital could supply, my dear.'

Macleod thought Stewart would start to find this creepy, but she smiled, albeit a brief movement of her muscles, almost short enough to be a spasm. 'Where are you staying, sir?' asked Macleod.

'Oh, I have a small accommodation just up and round from here, I can walk back. But first let me buy the both of you a drink. Bloody good show from the pair of you. Many people criticize the police, but I never have; even when I've been on the end of the long arm, I've never said a bad word about them.'

Macleod noted the rather dapper suit of the man and the shoes that spoke of class, bought in some upmarket shop. His own were expensive for he was on his feet a lot, but these actually looked smart too.

'Whisky all round, I think,' he said and when Stewart put up her hand, he grabbed it, saying he insisted and kept hold of the hand. 'An angel indeed. But a devil to fight, eh? Where did you find such a woman, sir?'

Macleod reckoned he was in a sitcom and this was the daft, rich uncle whose lurid words were tolerated and laughed at as he was a harmless fool. But Macleod knew nothing about this man.

'What's your name, sir, just for the record.'

'Alan Dickerson, from Kent. Up here for a look round the fairer parts of this magnificent country. But I never expected to see such beauty as this. And a magnificent specimen like yourself, sir. Obliged to the both of you. Now, drink this with me.'

A tray of whiskey had arrived, double shots all round and Macleod was cajoled into accepting the glass. The man had bought a round for everyone in the room and looked to everyone to take their glass altogether. 'Right, one, two, three, and down the hatch.' The room as one dropped their drinks and the charismatic Englishman got to his feet.

'Time for bed,' he said, 'but thank you all. And especially to you, my dear,' said the man as Stewart stood up. He placed a hand on her cheek and then looked as if he was going to give her a kiss on the lips. Stewart dropped her head and he ended up kissing her on the forehead.

'I'll get someone to drop you home,' said Macleod, 'and then you can make a statement tomorrow at the station.'

'There's really no need,' said the man.

'Yes, there is,' Macleod replied. 'I insist.'

'Have it your way, sir. I'll be along tomorrow. Where is the station?'

'The constable who drives you home will tell you.' Macleod looked to the back of the room and the police officer who had been called by the bar staff. A simple nod came back, and Macleod indicated to the man that he wanted an address from wherever they ended up tonight.

And two minutes later the bar had almost emptied. Macleod had sat down and Stewart was beside him. 'Time for bed, Stewart, long day tomorrow again.'

'Yes sir, do you need any help?'

'I'm not an invalid, Stewart. Just took a bad punch.'

'Of course, sir.'

The pair made their way out of the bar and to their bedrooms which were beside each other. As they reached them, Macleod turned and looked at Stewart. 'Are you okay? You took a few good hits out there.'

'Nothing I don't take in the ring. You know I do martial arts, don't you?'

'You certainly have the skills, Stewart. The man was extremely impressed anyway.'

He saw Stewart go to adjust her glasses but then refrain due to their absence. 'Dirty old bastard, sir. He was looking right down my top when I was kneeling. I don't normally go around like this, but he made sure he got his money's worth for the view.'

'You could have changed. Sorry, but I didn't realise you were so uncomfortable. You seemed to be okay with it—I even saw you smile once.'

'The man was in shock and beaten up. I didn't need to give him a row about appropriateness.'

'That was magnanimous of you, Stewart. What about your glasses?'

'I have a spare pair, sir. I'll bill the force.' And she smiled, without any sign that it was forced. 'As long as you are okay.'

'I am. Thank you. I appreciate it, Kirsten.' Macleod saw her face light up and she beamed before turning to her door.

'Goodnight, sir.' He watched her open the door, her gown now pulled tight around her and her bare legs underneath. He knew the feelings that were coming into his head and he rebuked them. Kirsten was quite something, and as a person he found her intriguing and refreshing despite her apparently closed nature. Until tonight he had not really noticed her figure. That was a lie—he had, but he had not dwelt on it. And he should not dwell on it now either. There was nothing untoward in his fondness for her as long as it stayed there. *Get a grip, Seoras; there's a killer to catch.*

Chapter 5

Macleod rose early for breakfast, unable to sleep, and then stood outside the hotel in rather dreich weather for half an hour mulling over his thoughts. Contacting the local police, he found out the address that they had dropped Alan Dickerson off the previous evening. As he pondered if the incident was in any way connected to the body on Vatersay, he heard a cough behind him.

'Ah, Stewart, up nice and early, or could you not sleep like me? I'm afraid once the bit is between my teeth, I don't rest easy until we solve the case. Bad habit for a policeman, I know.'

'Are you feeling okay, sir?' asked Stewart.

Macleod saw the shiner just around her eye, hidden partially by the glasses. 'Am I feeling okay? Well yes, but are you okay? I mean, that looks like quite a bruise around your eye.'

Stewart pushed the glasses back onto the nose. 'I'm fine, get worse in the ring.' Wearing a smart pair of black trousers, boots, a tight, thin jumper and a designer leather jacket, Stewart looked the part of a senior detective and much changed from Macleod's first meeting with her. Maybe she was trying to copy Hope, which was a pity if correct, as she had no need, as her own style suited her well.

'If you're sure. I thought we should take a quick run round

to Mr Dickerson before we start today. I have a nagging doubt about him, a little too keen to just go home, and also the round of drinks for everyone. Bit over the top for a man who's been mugged.'

'I was going to say, sir. By the way I have the hire car for us, not that the island is that large. Do you want me to drive? McGrath says you usually like your partner to drive.'

Macleod nodded and Stewart showed him to a small three-door car. 'They didn't see the need for something too large,' she said, 'what with our environmental considerations and that.' Macleod did feel the need for more leg room but he said nothing and watched the green, undulating hillocks that they spun by, making the houses appear at odd angles perched at the roadside. Like his Lewis home, there was plenty of water around and they saw the iconic Kisimul Castle as they passed along the shore at Castlebay.

The lonely, stone fortress stood huddled from the misty drizzle alone in the bay. It was the sort of place Jane would like, somewhere to drag Macleod round and explain the history to him. History was inevitably filled with blood feuds and murder so Macleod had a natural aversion to these sorts of trips believing he saw enough of that type of carry-on in his own work.

A winding road ran for almost three kilometres before Stewart took a turnoff that led to the shore and a small bay. There were a number of houses, well-spaced apart and each plonked neatly beside the single-track road. The ground was full of wild and wet, green grass with the occasional rock jutting out through the lush vegetation. A power cable broke the idyllic picture-postcard image but Macleod thought it looked perfect. Solitude with just enough neighbours and the water to walk by at all times. It was like Lewis but had its own distinct character. And being further south, it might even get a touch warmer.

Small rivulets ran to the sea beside the houses and broke up their land, necessitating the erection of small bridges here and there. And Macleod thought the decision to have Stewart drive was a splendid one due to the narrow turns involved.

'We're here.'

How did Stewart know that? thought Macleod. He had not told her the address, so she must have been on the telephone to the local force too. The girl was too damn efficient. *Woman, Seoras, woman!* He was getting too old—they all seemed like boys and girls now in the force to him.

Striding up to the front door of the house, Macleod noted it was a holiday let, indicated by the sign adjacent to the driveway. With practised ease, he knocked politely but firmly with a sound that reverberated in the morning still. No one replied and he rapped the door again. It opened and a young man of over six foot looked down at Macleod. He was standing in a pair of boxer shorts and nothing else and had very bleary eyes.

'God, what's the crisis, skipper?'

'DI Macleod and DC Stewart, sir. My apologies for disturbing you at this early hour but we are looking for a Mr Alan Dickerson who advised us he was living at this address. Is he at the house?'

'Alan who? Never bloody heard of him.' He turned round and called out. 'Faith, you ever heard of an Alan Dickerson.'

A black woman walked down the hallway behind the man and stood at his shoulder. She was in a crop top and pants and Macleod felt he should look away but instead tried to keep the impassive police face that he had borne to many a situation in his life.

'Never heard of an Alan Dickerson, Colin. Should I know him?'

Macleod focused on the man's face. 'Can I ask who you are and why you are here, sir? Just for the record.'

'Colin Masterton and she's Faith Keita, my partner. Just up to get away from things. We both work in London and this is a break from the grind. A little together time.' The man passed his address to Macleod.

'Well, sorry to bother you, sir,' said Macleod, 'I will leave you in peace but if a Mr Dickerson calls, please advise us on this number.' He handed the man a card with his details on it. 'Otherwise enjoy the day.'

'Oh, we will do that,' said Faith and stepped past Macleod into the drizzle. Her partner stepped forward and hugged her as they both smiled in the cool air. Stewart nodded towards the car and the two officers walked back to their vehicle. As they drove away, the young pair were still standing there in their underwear, eyes closed and smiling. Apparently, the accursed dreich weather, which so often annoyed islanders, was a welcome change to the London pair.

'Nice body,' said Stewart as she steered the car back to the main road to Castlebay.

'Yes, she was quite lovely but she really could have worn a bit more.'

'I was talking about him, sir.'

'Of course you were, Stewart.' An awkward silence reigned while they travelled the short distance back to the small police station. Inside, Macleod found the local constable and advised him of the deception carried out by Mr Dickerson, although Macleod now doubted that was his real name. The constable said he would look into it and Macleod turned to some reports he was given on the murder scene. As he was sitting reading, Mackintosh appeared before him, her eyes looking puffy with large bags beneath them making her look her years for once.

'Mackintosh,' said Macleod, almost proud of using her surname, 'what's the deal with the body?'

'He was knifed in the back and it was done by someone who knew how, as well. Probably taken by surprise which would have been impressive on that beach. He was murdered there as far as I can tell although a lot of sand tracks were washed away by the tide and the body had been moved a short distance by the recovering team. I have DNA samples, and the usual, away for confirmation of identity but who knows.'

'Thanks, Mackintosh, has it been an all-nighter?'

'Yes, Seoras, it has, but happy to do it for you, as ever.' There was a flicker of a smile but the woman looked simply shattered. 'Heard you got a bit of a beating last night. Are you okay?'

Looking up, Macleod saw a genuinely worried look on the woman's face. This was what was so difficult about Mackintosh. In his head he had an image of this lonely woman craving his body and attention but there was also a genuine care for him. He was certainly no piece of meat to her.

'I'm fine. Stewart took the brunt of it but she can handle herself. Mixed martial artist, apparently.'

'Well I'm glad you are okay. I'm going back to the hotel for a while but if you need me, just knock me up.' There was a moment's silence and they looked at each other uncomfortably. 'I mean feel free to wake me up, Seoras. God, I'm wrecked.'

'Thanks Hazel,' he said as she left the room. *Damn, I did it again.*

About an hour later, the local sergeant came to Macleod

with an address. 'I've been checking around the local hotel and guest house owners and there's one man matching Mr Dickerson's description staying in a hotel just on the edge of Castlebay. I've told the owner to expect you for a chat. Mairi Macleod, funny enough, sir. Take it she's not related.'

Macleod smiled but inside his mind was elsewhere. Why would a man of such an age need to lie about what he was doing? Only one way to find out and that was to find him, so he called for Stewart and they walked through the small village up to a house that sat on the edge of the bay looking out to Kisimul castle. It said hotel but really it was a large house which had been adapted and probably did not hold more than about eight guests. As they strode up the drive, a middle-aged woman with hair that was beginning to whiten opened the door and beckoned them inside.

'Hi there,' she said on their entry to the house. 'Can I get you a tea or coffee?'

'No thank you,' said Macleod, 'but you can tell me about the man the constable rang you about today, Mrs Macleod.'

'No, it's Mairi and bless my soul. I never seen one like as him.' The woman crossed herself and then looked to the wall where there was a crucifix. 'Who knows what the dear lord would make of him but I don't know.'

'Well. just start at the beginning, Mairi, and we'll take it from there,' said Macleod.

'Okay, Inspector. I got a phone call from a Mr Drummer six weeks ago, saying he would be needing some accommodation while up here and would I have room. Well at this time of year, who doesn't have room and I needed the money so I naturally accepted. He said he would pay cash and to add a little extra for that inconvenience.'

'Did he say why he was coming up?' asked Stewart.

'No, Never. And I didn't ask as I didn't want to turn away someone at this time of year. Well, he arrived a week ago and then had promptly vanished this morning but with the cash for the stay left on the bed and a note saying he had been in receipt of some bad news and needed to leave. I can show you the room but it's completely clear of all of his stuff.'

'Is it locked?' asked Macleod.

'No, I was just going to give it a clean and change the sheets.'

'Don't. Leave it be; don't enter it and lock it if possible. I'll be getting my forensic officer, Miss Mackintosh, over directly to you. While he was here, did you notice anything strange about him?'

'Well, no. He didn't eat here and was out in the morning by nine and not back until after ten at least. Very easy guest to look after. In fact, there was only the once I saw him having a barny with someone.'

'Who was that?' asked Macleod.

'Well, I didn't know him but he was a young man. They seemed to be discussing the fact that the young man had not received something, at least that's all I caught of it as they both clammed up once they saw me watching them. But it was about six at night and they disappeared off towards the harbour direction. When he came back that night, he had drunk a fair bit.'

'When was this?' asked Stewart.

'Two days ago.'

Macleod asked the woman to describe the young man and struggled to contain his excitement as it matched up to the man who he had tried to prevent from attacking Mr Dickerson/Drummer. Further questions revealed nothing else

45

and the detectives walked back to the station where Macleod asked Stewart to find out the drinking establishments in Castlebay and then meet him at the hotel. And then he walked to that hotel with an onerous task before him, the waking of Mackintosh.

Chapter 6

Hope stretched out her arms and yawned on the deck of the small ferry back to Oban. There was little else left to do on Canna now that the body had been recovered and was in the hands of the forensic team. All the islanders had been interviewed and little had been known of Jane Thorne on the island. There was also no help from the only tourists staying on the island—one of whom seemed more worried that their time away would get back to their university circle.

Ross was going to finish up and follow Hope over by tomorrow at the latest and she had chosen to take the ferry back rather than wait for the hired charter they had come in on. This was as much to get some thinking time to herself as anything else and also to check out the address for Jane Thorne in Oban. But it also meant she managed to call Allinson, her partner for the first time since she had raced out the door. At least call him for any sort of meaningful chat.

They were still in the earlier stages of their relationship and she found being away from him difficult in a physical sense. Indeed, when she managed to get through to him, he had asked for a video call, but the signal strength was not enough. Hope felt the disappointment as acutely as he did, and she wondered when she would get back up to Inverness.

As the ferry pulled into Mallaig, Hope ran through the options of what had happened to her victim. The woman was clearly killed by someone who could handle a knife but also who had strength, both to have held her but then also to have sliced right through the neck. There was a mental strength, or a detachment, in being able to watch the neck sever and then being able to watch the woman die in what would have been a gruesome death.

And what was Hope to make of the map that was found? The original was with forensics, but she had copies of both sides of the parchment and had stared at them on the ferry but to no avail. One side was just a map and the other incomplete instructions referencing places not on her map. The line of attack was going to be the address and her name, but the Oban police had said the address had proved fruitless as there was no one home. However, the neighbours had said they were a man and a woman, a quiet couple, who lived there.

Hope took her car along the winding road that cut inland towards Loch Linnhe before driving south towards Oban. The day was miserable, but the weather aside, the view was something else. She had travelled this way before and often thought of it as Scotland's forgotten coastline, a myriad of sea lochs and hills that took you far away from it all. Inverness was stunning on a good day nestled amongst the hills and the sea, but this was more intimate, every bend a small world of its own and then breaking into an extended view of the quiet loch. She should come here with Allinson—better than having a bikini selection argument in Greece.

Using the mapping app on her mobile, Hope found the address in Oban quickly after her long drive down from

Mallaig. It was on one of the small estates on the south side of Oban and occupied a space at the end of a cul-de-sac. The house was one of those modern builds and looked slightly smaller than the house next to it which had a double garage with both doors open showing an array of gardening equipment and children's bikes and toys. Outside a man was cleaning his car, a sporty number with low profile tyres and a badge on the bonnet to prove just how expensive it was.

Parking the car in the driveway of Jane Thorne's house, Hope opened the door and watched the man stop washing his car and look over at her. As she walked up to the door of the house, she felt him staring from over the small wooden fence that separated the properties. At the door, she rang the bell but heard no buzzer.

'They're not in,' said the man. 'My wife said they would be back today, but I've seen no sign.'

Hope nodded and peered into the hallway of the house. There was nothing of particular note inside, just a hallway like any other with a mirror on one side and a small alcove under the stairs where coats were hanging. She saw both male and female coats and checked that off as this was their house. Whoever they were.

'Can I help you?' asked the man over the fence.

Hope turned around to see a beaming face and watched him puff himself up like some sort of peacock, ready to answer her call, poor maiden as she was. Striding over and producing her credentials from her back pocket, Hope had to stop herself from laughing at the man's attempt to sharpen his shoulders and pull in the small belly that was pushing at this t-shirt.

'Have you lived here long, Mr . . .?'

'Simon, Simon Rutledge. And yes, I've been here for eight

years.'

'On your own?'

'No,' said the man, shaking his head, 'The wife and I came here first and now we have two kids with us. I work as a fish-farm manager for my sins, Detective . . . ? I take it you are a detective?'

Hope laughed internally. *As opposed to what? Some random mad woman stalking houses.* 'Yes, sir, I am a detective, DS McGrath, and I'm interested in the owners of the property next to yours. You say they will be back today, or at least your wife says so. Do you know why she thinks that?'

'No, she just mentioned it.'

'Could you get her out her for me, sir?'

The man's face fell. 'Really? She's terribly busy, maybe I could help you, show you round the house. I've seen the couple a lot.'

I bet you have, Mr nosey parker. And I bet you've watched her. 'If you could please get your wife, sir, I really could do with speaking to her.'

Glumly, the man departed while Hope turned back to stare at the house. There was something about it that was bothering her. The couple had gone away and yet one bedroom window was cracked open slightly in what may have been an attempt to let some air through the place. But the other window at the upper floor of the house had its curtains closed. It was not particularly suspicious, but it seemed out of place with how neat everything else was.

Simon Rutledge returned with his wife and this time acted as if Hope was nothing special at all, gazing away from her the whole time, leaving his wife to introduce herself.

'Hello, I'm Janine Rutledge. My husband says you're a

Detective?'

'DS McGrath, Mrs Rutledge. Your husband said you thought the couple next door would be back today; why is that?'

'I overheard them when they left. They only moved in four months ago and to be honest they are hardly ever here. Young types but very aloof. They never seem to be outside of the house when they are here, but I did notice that their house is somewhat warm.'

'Warm?' asked Hope. 'How so?'

'Well, I dropped round one day with a tray of shortbread to try and get to know them better and I managed to get invited into the kitchen. The weird thing was that she never said anything about herself. In fact, when her husband, or man—I don't know if they are married—he only referred to her as Bambi and she called him Thumper. I guess they just like their little pet names. Simon sometimes calls me his deer and he's my stag . . .'

'That's probably not what the detective wants to hear about, dear,' said the man going a bright red.

'Of course, Simon. But anyway, she was wondering around in a pair of pants and a t-shirt. And when he came into the kitchen, and it was only briefly, he only had a pair of boxers on. It was quite a sight, but I don't think they had been up to anything or I had interrupted them. It was just so warm. I was sweating just sitting in there.'

'And they never said their names to you?' asked Hope.

'Never. But it was strange, don't you think, the house being so warm.'

'And do they dress that way often?'

'The woman hardly ever wears anything else,' said Mr Rutledge and received a stare from his wife. 'Hey, it's not my fault she dresses like that.' He turned back to Hope. 'She goes out to the shed at the back of the house about four times a day. My wife is right, always dressed that way.'

'Four times a day,' asked Hope. 'Were these times regular?'

'Yes, seven in the morning, midday, four in the afternoon and then about eight at night.'

'And those are rough times,' said Hope trying not to smile, 'and always in pants and a t-shirt.'

'Always,' said Mr Rutledge and Hope saw the anger in the woman's face.

'You used to shove me into the shower at seven, no bloody wonder.'

'You were the one getting a full view of boxer-shorts man. You never told me that.'

'Easy,' said Hope. 'I have something more important on at the moment.' But her words were drowned out by a car pulling up to the driveway behind her own car. As the engine died, the occupants seemed to sit for a while before the driver's door opened and a tall, tanned, white man stepped out and pulled off a pair of sunglasses to look over at Hope. *Sunglasses,* Hope thought, *we're having to hunt for the sun.*

'Is there a problem?' asked the man stepping round the car and Hope saw why Mrs Rutledge had not told her husband about the boxer shorts. The man was in great shape and had one of those chiselled chins that was covered with a moderate amount of stubble. The other door swung open and a dark-haired woman of maybe twenty stepped out in a pair of jeans and a white t-shirt. Again, Hope got why Mr Rutledge sent his wife to the shower. These two certainly looked the part.

'DS McGrath, sir. I need to have a word with you about your house; it's in connection with an investigation I'm running.

Just routine, nothing to worry about. If we could go inside.' The heat in the house was making Hope wonder just what was happening but she needed to retain her focus on her primary reason for being there.

'Come this way,' said the woman and did not stare at her neighbours once. Similarly, the man walked off without a word, but they went to the side of the house and beckoned Hope to follow.

'Thank you, Mr and Mrs Rutledge, if I need anything else from you, I'll be in touch.' She watched their stunned faces, jaws dropped like some gawping goldfish. *There'll be a row in that house*, she thought. *Shoving her in the shower. What a guy!*

Hope was shown through the back door straight into the kitchen where a seat was pulled out for her. The room was like something from a brochure without a mark or any food on display. Hope wanted to open a few cupboards just to make sure something was inside them. But Mrs Rutledge had been right, and as Hope had walked through the door, she had been hit by a wall of humid moisture.

'You certainly like it warm,' said Hope.

'Yes,' said the man and Hope thought she heard an Eastern European accident, 'Bambi likes it hot, due to her South American roots. It's quite therapeutic, lets your pores cleanse.'

'Hell to sleep in, surely,' said Hope.

'How can we help you?' asked Bambi. Her voice was smooth and a little forced. *South American, my arse,* thought Hope.

'I have a body found on the isle of Canna and the deceased woman had documents that said she lived at this house. A Jane Thorne. Have you ever heard of the woman?'

The couple shook their heads. 'We only bought this house four months ago,' said Thumper and I don't recall the name of the seller being that name, although we did buy through an agent so it may have been.'

'Have you ever seen this woman? I apologise for the image, but we don't have any of her alive, so this is a sketch.' Again, they shook their heads. 'Okay, thanks for the information. I'm glad I caught you in.'

Hope showed herself out and once outside drove her car to the next street out of sight. She then opened the boot of the car and searched her bag for a new top and different pair of jeans. A baseball cap and the untying of her hair completed the quick change and she walked back round to the cul-de-sac.

Mr Rutledge had disappeared inside, no doubt explaining his viewing of his neighbour and Hope watched the front of the house as she approached it. There was no movement and she passed the car Bambi and Thumper had got out of. A quick sprint to the side of the house and then to the corner of the rear of the house. Hope checked her watch. Four o'clock. A few minutes later, out strolled the woman in pants and t-shirt, to the shed at the rear of the house.

Hope followed her quietly as she opened the door and stepped inside. Looking in from behind, Hope saw an array of pipework, gauges and electronic indications. There were temperatures, humidity readings and flowrates indicated as well as a large boiler in the rear of the shed.

'Would you like to explain what this is for?' asked Hope, causing the woman to spin round in shock. 'I think we should look inside the house. The woman's shoulders slumped, and she looked at the ground. 'Come on,' said Hope. *I guess I'm going to see Mrs Rutledge's stud in his boxers after all.*

Chapter 7

Alan Gilchrist stepped inside his four by four and turned the key in the ignition, sighing to himself. Last night had been rough. He did not know what was up with his wife but everything he did seemed to be wrong. Was it that time of life? Were her friends annoying her? Was it the kids? He had no idea but he did know that being out here about to drive around a beach was preferable to being at home today and so he thanked God for his small mercies as he crossed himself.

Picking up his handheld radio, he asked the control tower for permission to enter the runway. Having been given said permission, he drove out onto the white sand and looked at the receded tide. The small, twin-otter plane would be here in less than twenty minutes bringing some of the locals home and maybe the odd tourist, although at this time of year there would not be many. The walking wounded visiting the hospitals in Glasgow were more likely to be the main occupants.

Alan drove along the firm sand looking for anything unto-ward that would spoil an aircraft landing, his eyes sweeping here and there. Turning around, he looked up at Catherine in the control tower, her ears covered by large half domes but even from here he could see her smile. Everyone liked Catherine. The firemen, the manager, and Alan himself. She was twenty-five, blonde and bubbly but also more than capable of handling herself, be it with the fireman's banter or the occasional stubborn pilot. He used to think his wife was like that. Maybe underneath she still was but something had changed her over the years. Kids! That was it. Love them as he did, they left a scar.

A flash of light caught his eye from the grassy edge of the beach and Alan looked up at the sky to see the cloud cover broken into briefly. A shaft of light must have penetrated. It had caught something on the ground and Alan did his duty driving towards the FOD, or Foreign Object Debris as the manuals explained it. Stepping from the vehicle, Alan traipsed towards the grass before recoiling and falling to the sand. It could not be, surely. He forced himself back to his feet and looked again. Once more he was repelled, stumbling backwards, and collapsed onto the sand. Turning over he vomited on the unstained white sand and began to shed a tear. The radio sparked into life.

'Barra Information, OPS 1, come in. Barra Information, OPS 1, come in. Are you okay, Alan? Alan!'

Macleod stood with a coffee at the airport fire service unit awaiting the arrival of Mackintosh. He had made his way out to the body before leaving her to her devices and returning to the station to interview Alan Gilchrist. The man was nervous and difficult to get a proper statement from, but Macleod did not blame him. Murder was always horrible to look at but to have a head separated from a body was particularly nasty. Only his many years in the force had steeled him for the sight but he still felt somewhat queasy.

The reason Alan was in such a state, other than being confronted by a decapitated head, was that he knew the owner of that head. In fact, he had spoken to the man the previous night. On further investigation, everyone seemed to know the deceased man. A fact the Fire Chief was now recounting to Macleod.

'Dennis was an Englishman but nice enough for all that. Bit of a loner and happy to walk around the island late at night. Was a bit of a twitcher, liked his birds. You'd often see him out around the edges of the airport.'

Macleod nodded, looking out towards the beach. Something was bothering him about the murder. They had three dead now in a matter of days, and nothing to say there was any connection between the bodies. Had the islands just become the wild west? Was it a full moon? Of course not, so there must be some sort of connection. This amount of spilled blood did not happen here at this pace. At any pace, really.

'Do you know anything about Mr Parsons' past? Was Dennis up here for a reason?'

'Well, Inspector, he did not like to talk about his past, but I know he had some sort of major trauma, possibly military. He never spoke of it but Cath, up in the tower, she dropped him some food round once and he was asleep, crying out in his sleep. I think he had sleeping pills too.'

Macleod watched a Land Rover make its way towards the Fire Station and then stop before them. A fireman jumped out of the driver's seat before running around and opening the passenger door. Mackintosh hauled herself out of the vehicle and Macleod, usually on his best defence for the woman, just felt for her. She looked exhausted, battle-weary almost.

'Chief, can we use your office, please? I need to have a talk with Miss Mackintosh. And if it's not too much to ask, could we get her a coffee?'

The Fire Chief nodded and dispatched a fireman to the task before leading them into his office and pulling out a chair for Mackintosh. She fell into it and cursed at her feet. The Fire Chief smiled and then retired from the room shutting the door behind him.

'Are you having a special on bodies at the moment, Seoras? It's Barra of all places, idyllic Barra, battered by the weather but not this.'

Macleod nodded and gave a half smile. 'It is unusual, Hazel.' He knew he was using her first name, but he could not help but feel for her right now. She had been up working on the previous body, co-ordinating her team on Canna and now had been hauled from bed to see this new and even more gruesome site. 'But there's something troubling me about this one. How do we think he was attacked?'

'From behind by the looks of it. I have a footprint in the sand, partial because there is grass and vegetation underfoot which has obscured it somewhat, but you are looking at a boot. I'll get a tread image for you as soon as I can. It was a knife and I'm thinking it was similar to the one used on Canna in that it was a proper knife. But it would take a strong arm to remove the head while holding the person.'

'From behind quickly? Would the attacker have seen the face?'

'Doubtful in the moments of the attack. Previous to the moment, I can't say. Why?'

'I think this is a case of mistaken identity.'

'Bit of a jump, Seoras,' said Mackintosh and then nodded towards the door where a fireman stood behind it holding two cups of coffee. Macleod opened the door and thanked the man.

'As I was saying, bit of a jump, Seoras. Mistaken identity?'

'White hair, old, and with an English accent. I'm guessing it was a proper home counties accent, like Mr Dickerson or Drummer or whoever he is. Someone wants people dead. There's also the map found on our Canna body. I can't say for sure but given the timescale and this coincidence of my mystery man and our dead Mr Parsons, I believe there's something more going on than a few individual killings.'

Mackintosh sat up suddenly and yelped.

'Are you okay?' asked Macleod.

'My back's playing up, just around the shoulders. I can't reach it. It's blooming agony. Just a lack of sleep causing it but Jona's coming over today which will help. Of course, that's if you stop handing me more bodies.' Mackintosh flashed a smile which then turned into a wince of real pain.

Macleod walked round to the rear of Mackintosh's chair and placed his hands on her shoulders, driving his thumbs hard into the area under her blades. 'Don't take this the wrong way, Hazel, I'm just trying to sort your back.'

'I won't,' she said and then winced again.

'Sorry.'

'No, it's good, keep at it. If we had a less conspicuous office, I'd lie under some towels for you to do that, let you get at the skin properly.' Macleod's hands lifted slightly. 'I meant to get at the problem, Seoras, I wasn't coming on to you. I know you won't stray, which while a pity, is damn attractive. So, make sure you don't, or my dreams will be ruined.'

Mackintosh's familiarity bit at him but he continued his attentions to her shoulders, a trick that his partner Jane had taught him. Five minutes later and Mackintosh stood up, shrugging her shoulders.

'That's brilliant, Seoras, I could stay all day but there's work to do.' As she left the room, Mackintosh cast a long look back at Macleod before stopping at the door and saying, 'Take care.' And then she was off. Left standing, Macleod felt a pang of guilt but then told himself he was simply helping a colleague. *Better not make a habit of it.*

Before he could leave the Fire Chief's office, one of the local constables entered and advised they had some information about Dennis Parsons' movements last night. Macleod told the man to take a seat and then leant up against the main desk in the room.

'I asked Mr Parsons' neighbours if they had seen him last night and I have him leaving his house at seven before going to the Kisimul View Bar down at the bay. Apparently, he was in there for about three hours and spoke to a lot of people, but all local sir. I have the names if required. He left alone after borrowing a jacket from another man, strangely enough not a local but becoming one they said. A Mr Killarney. From there there's no sign of Mr Parsons until he was found dead today.'

'Killarney?' asked Macleod 'Did you get a description of Killarney?'

'A brief one, sir. White hair, English accent, very proper, quite old too. Apparently, he's been about for a few weeks now.'

Macleod stood up tall and wondered. 'Get back to the locals with a copy of the sketch made of our attacked man, Mr Drummer or Dickerson. See if Mr Killarney is him. Then see if anyone knows where he is. We need to find him and fast because I think his life is in danger.'

'Sir!' said the constable taking his leave.

He knows it too, Killarney, Dickerson or whoever he is, knows it, understands they are after him and offered up Parsons. But why are they after him, and the other victims?

Macleod decided to return to the station to co-ordinate efforts to find the still alive white-haired man but as he got close, he saw a number of journalists outside the building. Part of him wanted to walk away but he knew it was part of his job to deal with the vultures. And with two murders on Barra, as well as the one on Canna, the press would be having a field day.

'Inspector, Inspector,' came a cry as he stepped out of the car and walked towards the station, 'any news on the Highlander murders?'

Part of Macleod wanted to stop right there, take the man who had asked the question and simply slap him for inciting panic. *Highlander Murders!* It was the decapitated heads. He remembered the film and the premise, there could be only one or something like that. That was not the image required here.

'I will have a statement for you in due course,' said Macleod without a twitch on his calm exterior. 'Until then, please refrain from any wild speculation which may cause undue panic and agitation among the residents of this Island.'

'Do they use long swords to decapitate them, Inspector? Claymores?'

Macleod did now stop and eye up the man who had asked the question. Putting his right hand into his coat pocket, Macleod's fist clenched tight and his teeth started to grate but he controlled himself and gave a serious look to the journalists. 'As I said, there will be a statement in due course. If you will kindly excuse me and thank you for your time.' *Parasites, every last one!*

Chapter 8

Hope put the mobile phone into her pocket and shook her head. They were getting nowhere on the case, the Oban address having turned out to be a dead end, albeit one which highlighted a house where certain illegal substances where being farmed. It was certainly a positive on her record but it did not bring them any closer to finding the killer and that, as Macleod was always ready to say, was the only thing that mattered—not the awards, not the prestige. Only a killer behind bars.

Her mobile vibrated in her pocket again and Hope connected the call but did not recognise the number. Shaking her ponytail behind her, she put the device to her ear.

'This is DS McGrath.'

'Sergeant, this is Constable Finlay from Mallaig. I had one of the ferry crew on the Canna-Mallaig run drop into the station just now and give me a tale about a near fight on board the ferry that they saw. I was wondering if you wanted to interview them yourself. I've taken a statement but given the circumstances I thought you might want to speak to them directly.'

Macleod wanted Hope over to Barra as soon as possible and she had planned to catch the ferry from Oban across, but this was worth the trip back up to Mallaig. 'You're absolutely correct, constable, but it'll take me a few hours to get there, I'm in Oban. I'll see them this afternoon.

'Yes, ma'am, station will be open; come right on in.'

In the quieter parts of Scotland, the police stations were not always manned full time and Hope thought it took things back to a more familiar time and place where the local community was well known by the one and only local bobby. But the reality was not so quaint and although the service was often low in numbers in these parts, they were no less running a full service and responding in the same way as any other part of the force. It just took longer to get numbers to the more off-route towns and villages.

As Hope settled herself into the winding drive back to Mallaig, she took a call from Jona Nakamura, the forensic lead she was working with on Canna. 'Detective, Jona here, I've been called over to Barra to help out with circumstances there. I was wondering where you are at the moment as I had heard you were making for Oban. I'm due to catch the ferry from there in the morning after I wrap up a few details with the work from Canna.'

Hope smiled. During their brief room share on Canna, something had ignited between the women and she remembered Jona's ability to take the sting out of her shoulders and responsibilities. A bit of company would not go amiss.

'I'm making my way back up to Mallaig to interview someone,' said Hope, 'but I'm due on that ferry tomorrow too. I'll meet you tonight in Oban. If you're booking a hotel, get me a room.. What time are you expecting to get there?'

'Maybe eight, nine.'

'Well then, time for dinner and a glass or two of wine. See

you then.'

'Deal,' said Jona and cleared the call.

As the road swung this way and that among trees and the rare house, Hope realised she was looking forward to simply getting a break tonight even if it was just for a few hours. It had baffled her when Macleod seemed to allow Mackintosh to be a little closer to him than she thought necessary or even appropriate, given his relationship with Jane. But it was lonely being in charge and someone on the outside—and the forensics people were certainly on the outside, albeit they were also colleagues—was a perfect choice. And then her mind swung to Allinson back in Inverness. She had called him, but he was working and they had little chance to talk. But his effect was still there; she had just used the term appropriate in her thoughts about a relationship. Those were Allinson's, not Hope's.

The day remained dull and grey but the rain that had plagued her journey had stopped when she drove into the Mallaig and located the station. Inside she found Constable Finlay and he welcomed her by putting on the kettle before calling their witness on the landline. After a brief drink, a girl of maybe nineteen walked through the station front door dressed in black from head to foot. Her face was pale, but from applied make-up—and there was a tinge of purple around the eyes and on her lips.

Hope recognised a Goth when she saw one and the t-shirt underneath the long black coat showed the motif of a band she recognised. Thinking about her trip across to Canna, Hope did not recognise the girl, but she would have looked different.

'DS McGrath, this is Gail Curran, one of the crew from the Canna run and she dropped in to tell me a bit about an incident that happened on the boat the day before the body was found on Canna.'

'Thank you for coming in, Gail; please take a seat. Do you want a drink?'

The girl looked with cold eyes before shaking her head in the negative and then plonking herself like a falling sack of potatoes into the chair.

'Okay,' said Hope, 'just take it from the top, tell me everything you told the constable earlier on today and if I want to ask about something, I'll stop you. But otherwise just give me the whole tale. Okay?'

The girl pulled herself up to the table before her and looked over at Hope, seemingly studying her. For a moment, Hope wondered if she approved but the girl then dumped her elbows on the table and seemed to concentrate.

'It was a morning run and there were few people on the boat. The Master had asked me to clean out some of the toilets at the rear of the vessel and I was able to see out onto the rear passenger area, the one that's exposed to the elements. The rain was doing that drizzle thing, you know the one where it doesn't give up and gets you wet in no time. But I saw these two women. Well, one was older than the other.'

Hope pulled a photofit from her pocket of the dead woman at Canna and placed it on the table. 'Was the older woman this woman?'

The girl studied the picture for a moment. 'Definitely. That's her all right.'

'And what did the other woman look like?'

'She was a girl, not a woman, probably younger than me. In fact, definitely younger, maybe sixteen. Bit tarty looking, too. You know the type, bra strap showing. She's standing outside on a wet deck on the sea with the wind and drizzle but she's in her tight jeans and a crop top with the underwear showing. No class at all.'

Hope looked at the pale face and realised that there was a real loathing of this girl. Maybe Gail had suffered from these types of people as Goths often did. Gail was certainly not showing any flesh. Apart from her hands and face, there was no other white skin.

'So, what happened between them?'

'Well, the girl keeps pushing up against the woman and I think, looking back, she may have had a weapon in her hand, maybe a small knife or something like that because the woman kept looking at the girl's hand. I couldn't hear what they were rowing about, and it was definitely a row from their faces, but it seemed like the older woman was being accused of something.'

'How long did the incident go on for?'

'A few minutes and then the woman walked off. I didn't think anything of it but after that woman died and then I came off my rotation, I suddenly thought maybe there was something in what I saw, so I decided I should come in about it.'

'I'm glad you did, Gail. It's most helpful,' said Hope, thinking about what she should do. 'Just stay there a minute, Gail, I need to talk to the constable.' Hope took Constable Finlay to the front office and told him that DC Ross would be arriving with a sketch artist to make up an image of this young girl who threatened their victim. Hope advised she wanted it done that night and that Finlay was to make the arrangements with Gail Curran and also to pull together a full description of the young girl from Gail.

On walking back into the interview room, Gail looked up and smiled at Hope. 'I thought of something else. I said she looked a bit of slapper with her bra strap hanging out. Well, she also had a stud just under her lip. And she wore these large earrings, big hoops. She had black hair, bloody shiny and vibrant—lucky bitch—but it had these silver hoops falling in and out of it, hanging from her ears.'

'Anything else about her?' asked Hope.

Gail suddenly looked downwards before lifting her face with a sullen look. 'Yeah, I don't think it was her bra doing it, but she was bloody lucky with her boobs. Big for her age, I reckoned. I remember because, Alex said it to me when he saw her coming on board.'

'Did she have a car?'

'No, I think she walked on. But she was pretty happy with her looks. Shed load of make-up on too. Spider eyes because of the mascara, fake tan I reckon, arse out, boobs shoved forward. Little tart.'

'Alex, you said, who's Alex.'

'The main cook. Romanian, blond-haired, and into good music.'

Hope saw beyond the comment and reckoned Alex and Gail may have spent more than work time together at sea. No wonder the girl seemed a threat to Gail. 'Are you going anywhere tonight, Gail?'

She shook her head in the negative and Hope smiled. 'Good, I have a friend coming down to this station tonight, a DC Ross who will want to speak to you. He's going to bring an artist with him to see if we can get a good likeness of the girl you saw. Constable Finlay will advise you of the time. Also, if you have Alex's number, can you give it to the constable?'

Less than twenty minutes later, Hope was back on the road heading for Oban. She had called Ross and explained the situation, giving him instructions for the night. Macleod had already been onto her, advising that Ross should man the main office when he was complete, and that Hope was to get over to Barra first thing.

Her shoulders ached and she fought fatigue on the way as her mind raced through possible options about the young girl who was on the ferry. But she had not gotten off the ferry at Canna; that was established by the ferry records. There was also something nagging her about the case on Barra too—was it connected? Macleod must have the same idea as he was asking for her to be with him while this was a murder investigation in its own right. And what was the whole map deal?

After arriving at her hotel and changing into a pair of jeans and a loose t-shirt, Hope sat with a glass of wine at a seat overlooking the entrance to the hotel. At ten o'clock, Jona Nakamura walked up the hotel steps and checked in at reception. Hope waved and then waited ten minutes while the Asian woman went to her room and deposited her bags. By half past ten, they were eating together from the twenty-four bar menu.

Hope felt exhausted but she listened to Jona talking about her day and then about her mother, who was apparently threatening to come up north and sort out her daughter. Jona was of an age for marriage, it seemed, and the family was keen to make it happen.

'This is the UK and here, it's my choice,' she said and showed a determined face with it.

'You tell them,' said Hope and felt a warmth towards the woman. She was certainly easy to look at and her smile lit Hope up inside. But all too soon the evening had gone, and the plates were cleared. Tomorrow was an early start and Jona wanted some sleep. Hope did not blame her, and she knew she could do with some herself.

The room was hot and as Hope lay beneath the covers, she could not get comfortable despite being in her bare skin as she always slept. There was something making her leg itch, and then her shoulders would not sit comfortably in any position. Macleod would want progress on the case tomorrow. No, her case. She rang Allinson but got no reply.

Hope got out of bed and threw on her dressing gown. Outside her window the rain kept coming and she looked at the streetlights, their beams blurred through the raindrops. She should not bother anyone but just accept she was restless and try and get back to bed. But Hope picked up her key card and stepped out into the corridor and walked five rooms along. She gave a gentle knock.

'Yes, who is it?' came a tired voice.

'It's Hope, can I come in?'

'It's three in the morning; what's the crisis?'

The door opened and Jona stood in a pair of pyjama bottoms, long and blue, along with a t-shirt that showed a crazy duck motif. Hope smiled and Jona forced a return, but she was clearly not happy. 'Come in.'

'Sorry to bother you but it's just, I can't get to sleep. I'm just lying there all tense and all I can do is think about things. I just needed to come and see you.'

Jona's face was serious, and a little angry. 'You stared at me all night at dinner and now you come into my room in just a dressing gown at three in the morning. I need to know, Hope, is this some sort of a half-assed come on.'

Hope's face collapsed into a look of horror and then she thought about the evening before crumbling into laughter.

'Sorry, it would look like that, I never thought. I'm just sore and restless and over on Canna when you worked your magic on my back it took it all away. I was just wondering if you could do that again.'

'Lie down on the bed,' said Jona, the grin returning to her face. 'Of course, I can. You had me worried. I'm not into girls that way.'

Hope lay on the bed and found her gown being removed before a pair of angelic hands performed a massage that went from brutal to relaxing in a matter of minutes. It was so good. Imagine her thinking I was coming on to her. And Hope remembered how she had sat with her wine watching the car park for Jona's arrival. And then listening to every word at dinner. And a thought struck her. There was something in what Jona said; she had come on but not intentionally. She'd need to make sure it did not happen again. Jona was ready to be a proper friend by the look of it, and she did not want to blow that.

Chapter 9

'**A**re they all gathered?' asked Macleod looking at Stewart with ever increasing tiredness in his eyes. 'Just rounding up the last of them, sir, but they will be there by the time you've been through the others.'

'Just make sure they are.' He snorted in frustration but then saw Stewart slowly move her glasses up her nose and fix him with a steely eye. 'Sorry, Kirsten. Of course, you'll have it sorted. It's just this damn case. Three dead and we have nothing, just about nothing. Except a dead local who didn't deserve to die. I'm just tetchy.' He grinned at her and saw the eyes soften. 'This is what McGrath deflects away from the rest of you,' Macleod said in a conciliatory gesture.

'I'm sure you're right, sir,' replied Stewart in a voice that said she was not.

Stewart left Macleod alone in the back room of the small police station and he picked up the file in front of him. The scene at Barra airport was there in a collection of photographs that seemed grimmer every time he looked at them. *Poor man, deliberately used. That's what I'm here to stop, that's my job. If these animals want to kill each other that would be one thing, but this man had nothing to do with it.*

Stewart arrived back in the room with a steaming cup

of coffee and placed it in front of her boss. Thanking her, Macleod lifted it to his lips and took a long slow drink while ignoring the scalding effect on his tongue. *Yes, that was the one. A cup never goes amiss when the pressure's on.* Setting the cup down and looking back up, he saw Stewart watching him, her smart black jacket lying open and a cream blouse neatly worn underneath gave no indication of the fight she had been involved in two nights ago. But the bruising on her face did.

'Just doing what McGrath would do, sir. Need to keep you on the boil.'

Smiling, she turned away and Macleod felt that fondness again that struggled to stay on the side of appreciative boss and not descend into a more primal feeling. It was easier in the old days all right; he had never had these feelings about his staff and colleagues then. Except Mrs Gordon in the typing pool, but he was in his twenties then and she was a mature older woman whose marriage was on the rocks. Her eyes had said all and he enjoyed the feeling, but he had never once said anything to her or anyone about what had gone through his mind. *Changed days. My mind might still think like that but I doubt the body could handle a Mrs Gordon.* Macleod laughed to himself and then felt guilty; his mind should not be on such frivolous things when there was a murder hunt to conduct.

The customers from the bar, who last night were enjoying a quiet drink or two before finding out that their friend was dead the following morning, were assembled in the same locale. The smell of stale beer and the previous night's sweat in the small room hung like a testimony to the worst hangover they had ever experienced, one alcohol was not responsible for. Macleod saw sullen faces and even the odd tear being cast. This was not going to be an easy session of interviews. Macleod

73

asked the assembled crowd of eight people not to talk to each other but to wait in the bar while he called them through one by one. After being spoken to they would be free to go, for the local constable had vouched that all of the customers were locals from the island.

Macleod walked through to a second room and sat behind a desk Stewart had laid out before the woman walked through with their first witness, an elderly man of maybe seventy. His hair was not white but grey and maybe that had been his good fortune because otherwise he was a perfect cover for the man with a thousand names, as Macleod was starting to think of their suspect.

'James Smith,' said Stewart who, after offering the old man a seat, sat down herself beside Macleod. The interview lasted less than ten minutes. He had seen the white-haired stranger and the description given matched perfectly. The man had moved around the bar, talking to everyone, offering drinks that were duly accepted. The same story came from the next five customers as well. Then came a young man of sixteen.

'This is Iain John Mackenzie,' said Stewart, after bringing the nervous young lad through.

'Hello, Iain,' said Macleod, trying to appear relaxed, but his unease at such a young lad being caught up in the affair was palpable. 'What were you doing in the pub last night?'

'I popped in to pick up a tipple for my Gran. It was late and she wanted something before she went to bed. She lives with us, you see, and Mum was already in her dressing gown, so I got sent out.'

'Dad not around?'

'Fishing on a trawler, not due back until Friday.'

'Did you see anything unusual last night? I assume this is

74

not the first errand like this you have run for your Gran.'

The boy coughed. 'I usually end up popping in for her two to three times a week. She could get something from the shop to keep her going but this is the only place that does her brand of milk stout. I don't get it because there's hardly any alcohol in it, but she insists. I don't mind because I get a wee drink while I'm here.'

Macleod raised his eyebrows.

'Nothing like that, mister. Just a wee coke or an Irn Bru. Once I did get a beer. Well, a shandy. Seemed like a lot of lemonade.'

'That's fine, Iain, but did you see anything unusual?' asked Stewart, focusing the boy.

'Well, that bloke was in, the white-haired oldie. Bought me a drink actually. He was talking with everyone, seemed quite happy. That's all I saw except for the envelope he gave Dennis.'

'Envelope?' started Macleod. 'What envelope?'

'It was really subtle, like in the movies but I was looking at him directly and saw it being passed just under the table. I doubt you would have seen it from any other direction, but he saw me looking at him, the white-haired guy and he put his finger up, telling me to shush.'

'And then what?'

'Then the milk stout was placed on the bar and I left.'

'And did you see what was in the envelope?'

'No,' said Iain, 'but it was brown, and seemed pretty packed.'

'What size?' asked Stewart.

'Not the letter type. About twice that size but not massive. Like half a piece of paper.'

After checking his statement again, Macleod asked the boy to wait with the constable on duty and turned to Stewart. 'You need to keep an eye on him; he's seen the exchange and our Mr Dickerson or Drummer knows. It links Drummer to setting Dennis up to be killed. Makes whoever did it think it was Drummer and not Dennis. The kid could be in danger.'

'I'll sort it directly after, sir. I'll get the last one, shall I?'

Macleod nodded and Stewart brought through a nervous woman. She was wearing an opened overcoat, but underneath was a dress that fought against the gloom of the outside weather. *About two seasons out*, thought Macleod. The woman's blonde hair was in a mess, tangled, and looked as if it had not been brushed this morning and her make-up was smudged, and if he was not mistaken given he was no expert with this sort of thing, it looked like last night's.

'Miss Elaine MacIver, sir.' Looking up at him, the woman nervously pushed at her hair revealing a lazy eye and a scar across her cheek. It was old but deep.

'So, Elaine,' said Stewart, 'tell us what happened last night.' The woman was shaking and began to look around her before starting to sniff. 'It's only an interview,' said Stewart, 'no need to get upset. Just tell us what happened here last night. Was Mr Parsons your friend?'

Breaking down completely, Elaine swooned and then fell to the floor. Macleod was out of his seat and began to lift her up but saw the eyes rolling in the woman's head. With Stewart's help, they got her back in the chair, but she then leaned forward and began to throw up. Macleod stepped to one side but his shoe was caught in the flow of puke and he reared at the smell of it.

'I didn't know,' Elaine spat through her rapid gulps for air, globules of stinking spit falling from her mouth. 'He didn't say. I was just lonely.'

'Who?' asked Stewart, but the woman vomited again, this time hard and dry as the stomach fought to find something to eject.

Macleod grabbed Elaine's shoulder and shook her gently. 'Who?'

'Eric Drummer!' she yelled. 'I fucking shagged him!' Again, the woman started to fall and Macleod reached forward ignoring the vomit and general mess of the woman and caught her. 'Constable!' he cried, seeking assistance. After a moment's spitting and then an attempt to wipe her hair with a puke covered hand, Elaine seemed to focus for a moment.

'You said to come here. When I told him, he never said, just lay there, telling me how beautiful I looked as I got changed. Let me walk out the door and never said about Dennis. Sweet Dennis.'

'Is he still there?' Elaine said nothing but started sniffing again. 'Is he still there?' shouted Macleod at the woman. Raising her head, she nodded. 'What's your address?'

'I know the house,' interjected the local constable and Macleod turned to Stewart.

'Hold the fort here, Stewart.' With that Macleod pointed at the constable, his finger wagging in a go motion. The smell of puke followed Macleod, mainly due to it being on his arm and shoes but he was suddenly alive, like a young one again. He followed the constable through the bar and out into the street with the smell of the sea rolling into his nostrils. The younger officer stretched the gap somewhat as they ran uphill and around a corner to a small cottage.

'Go,' shouted Macleod. The constable tried the door which was open and stepped inside. Macleod followed and together then raced through the house but there was no sign of anyone still being there. In the bedroom, Macleod bent over and tried to catch his breath while he looked around. The only clothes were female. He saw no bags and nothing that said anyone but Elaine McIver lived here. But then he looked at the bed with its disturbed undersheet and the smell of sweat coming from it. Looking closely, he saw stains although he could not identify exactly what they were. But they were of last night, he was sure of it.

Grabbing his mobile, he tapped Mackintosh's face on the small icon and held the device to his ear.

'Can you not let me get a moment's peace?' said a voice that was being playfully annoyed.

'I have something for you, Mackintosh,' he said, 'the trail just warmed up again.'

Mackintosh stood in her white coverall looking down at the bed. With a pointed finger, she motioned to the dressing table and wardrobe, sending one of her colleagues towards them while another brought in evidence bags. Standing beyond the bedroom in his own coverall, Macleod saw the woman's exhausted face, the features taut where they were usually rounded if a little worn. One hand was on her hip which was popped out to one side. Although not tall, the woman had presence in abundance but now her shoulders were slumped. It made him wonder about her life outside of work; did she have one? She never mentioned anyone else, and only referred to her younger colleagues.

Having instructed her team on their jobs, Mackintosh walked past Macleod with one finger held up, curling it in a follow-me motion and walked out of the house. Outside the drizzle had given up for the moment, but the sky was still grey and a light breeze blew.

'Semen, sweat, hair of all the varieties. I should be able to get you some DNA and then we can see if we can get a match. Bit sloppy of him really, don't you think?'

Mackintosh breathed deeply like today was an effort just to keep going. Along her forehead there were lines of worry that did not belong and Macleod wondered if she was a little distracted.

'So how long do you reckon?'

'Give me a pissing chance, Macleod. For frig's sake, I've only got the team here.' The reply was brutal, the eyes wild as she said it and Macleod actually recoiled a little.

'Okay, calm down. I know we're in a race what with the number of bodies but keep your head, Hazel.'

'What would you know? Perfect little wife at home, second chances just fell your way. I don't even have time for mine.'

Macleod felt angry that Jane was being brought into the conversation, but his instincts said something was wrong. In the old days you would have just coughed and stepped away but today you had some sort of right to pry, to make sure your colleague was okay.

'Come over here,' said Macleod, and took Mackintosh by the arm to the side of the house away from all eyes. 'What's the matter, Hazel? This is not you. I know we're busy, but this is not how you tackle work. What else is happening?'

The woman stared up at Macleod, her eyes gazing on his face like he had just asked the one question no one knew to ask. A hand was raised and touched his cheek as her eyes began to blink before tears started.

'Cancer, Seoras, they found cancer. Confirmed it today. I don't want to die, Seoras. Not yet—I'm not ready.'

He grabbed her and pulled her close letting her head rest

on his chest. Feeling her shudder and let everything out, he gripped tight whispering, 'It's okay; I've got you.' The drizzle started again and he wondered how long they would stand there. Then he felt her arms wrap around him.

'I need someone to help me through this. I have no one, Seoras, no one. You understand?'

His mind returned to the water just outside of Stornoway, to his wife disappearing below the surface having stepped out into the blue of her own free accord, leaving him. With the nature of her death and the belief at the time surrounding those who took their own lives, he had been pitied but not supported in the way he needed. No one had mentioned her actions or where she would go on to. Discussion of heaven had gone quiet when heaven itself had fallen silent and he needed someone to share it all with. He had never had cancer or seen any loved one taken by it, but he understood pain and loneliness combined, and he understood that panic, that fear of not knowing.

'I'll help you,' he whispered; 'you have me.' He held her for a moment longer until they heard someone just around the corner of the house. Mackintosh straightened up and wiped her eyes dry just before one of her colleagues brought her an evidence bag to look at. When they had departed, Mackintosh stared at Macleod, her eyes still sullen but there was a faint smile on her lips.

'Thank you. I won't ask for more than a friend would ask for. I understand you are attached. But I need someone, Seoras. It's . . .'

'Terrifying.' She nodded and walked away. Macleod stood and felt a tear forming in his eye. All his life he had seen death and misfortune, but Mackintosh's plight was cutting him to the core. Yes, she was a colleague and that was painful, but he understood she was under his skin in other ways. He would have to tread lightly, not that he thought she would deliberately take any liberties. But he understood how emotions ran riot when pressure was on, when the world went to pot. And Mackintosh's world would struggle to seem any worse.

'Sir,' said Stewart. It was like she had appeared from nowhere. Macleod panicked inside and wondered if she had seen Mackintosh and himself. Would he have to explain? Stewart was so good at seeing through the trees. 'Sir, I did some checking up on Karen Gibbons, our first informant. While she has a clean bill of health, her mother is more of a dark horse. She has previous for theft, quite a long record in fact, caught up in some large heists usually working as a team with several others. I know she's seventy plus now, but I thought given the age of some of the other characters we are looking for, it was worth investigating.'

'Absolutely, go and see if you can get any more from them directly, Stewart. Also chase up with the local force whether anything has come from checks around our first victim's known acquaintances and life on the mainland. There's a connection we are missing here, Stewart.'

Macleod saw the glasses being pushed up onto her nose and wondered what was coming next.

'I'd like to make a request, sir.' Macleod nodded. 'I want to go to the mainland to see if I can track down something in the mainland lives of these people myself. I reckon that's where the real tale is, sir. Whatever's happening is happening here but the story is not; it's in the past and on the mainland. Let me go and chase it up.'

'Why, what do you have?' asked Macleod.

'Just suspicions, sir.'

'Not until McGrath gets here, Stewart. Then I'll consider it. There's going to be more media coming and I need a team right here. We're stretched as it is.'

'Sir,' and the glasses went back up again.

Kirsten Stewart was a little ferret, Macleod knew that and to let her loose was an idea that had merit but Kirsten was also raw, inexperienced and she needed to be careful when going into the past, especially if it was a secret the treasure seekers intended to keep. It was hard to think as Mackintosh's face—the pain of her eyes—was still burning in his mind. His mobile rang. *Not the boss, there's enough to do!*

Chapter 10

Hope cursed the rain as she stepped from the car and made for the hotel where the team were staying. Jona Nakamura followed in behind her and the two women stood at the reception desk before hearing a shout from a short distance away. Macleod was waving her over and she saw the usually bustling figure of Mackintosh beside him, but she was rather subdued. Pointing them out to Jona, Hope walked over to the small table and sofa the pair were sitting at and noticed the whiskey in front of Mackintosh. There were two glasses as well as Macleod's coffee.

'McGrath, glad you're here, I need you to get settled in quickly as I have a job for you tonight. And before you complain, I've been through the ringer over here.'

Raising her eyebrows, Hope thought about pointing out how she had been legging it round the small isles running a case of her own but she saw the tiredness in Macleod's body, his slumped shoulders which he never had unless exhausted. He was also keeping company with Mackintosh on his own so things must have been grim.

It took Hope ten minutes to remove her things from the car, check in, and return to the table, Jona mirroring her actions. In that time Macleod and Mackintosh had not moved and indeed the head forensic examiner had another whiskey before her.

'Miss Nakamura,' said Macleod, 'I believe I have only seen you in passing but your presence is most welcome. As of now until further notice, you will be our main point of contact. Unfortunately, Miss Mackintosh is feeling somewhat under the weather and although here should you require her, we will be coming to you for all our forensic needs.'

Hope watched Jona's face become slightly suspicious and then look at Mackintosh who simply nodded at her. 'You two had best get a handover,' advised Macleod, 'I'll just have a word with my sergeant in private.'

Macleod took Hope by the arm and walked her to a different table. 'It is good to see you, Hope,' he said offering her a seat, 'but I'm afraid it's going to be a busy night for you. We are way understaffed here and Mackintosh is not feeling right. In fact, I have advised her to get to bed soon as possible. On our side of the case, I need you to keep an eye on Karen Gibbons, our first informant for the murder on Vatersay.'

'You know I still have my own investigation going for Canna?'

'And I reckon they may be one and the same. I take it Ross is following up the mainland leads, such as there are any for that murder.'

'Of course he is, as was I. Now I'm here, it's up to him.'

'Good, because Stewart's in bed and on the first plane out tomorrow. She thinks she can get into what's going on by tracing our murdered man's contacts on the mainland. I reckon it's a long enough shot, if any are still about, but she's the sort of person who can ferret that sort of thing out.'

'And I wouldn't have been. You could have kept me on the mainland and I could have done it as well as working with

Ross on the Canna murder. Now I'm doing everything by telephone with him.'

'You're being a bit protective over this. Besides, I need you undercover watching Karen Gibbons. I think she's here for a reason and she already knows Stewart and myself. So that's your task tonight. Here's her hotel address and details, photographs of her and her mother, although I doubt the old woman will be running around anywhere much. I don't buy her cover story of the sudden affair. Her mother's an old customer of ours as well so I think we need to keep a close eye.'

Hope grimaced. 'Okay, I'll take Jona with me for the earlier hours of the evening as we came over on the ferry together and we may be seen as friends, but I'll get her back here by midnight. I'm sure she has lots to do.'

'She'll have plenty. Mackintosh is not well at all. So only if Jona's okay with it should you take her.'

'Of course, sir. I'll advise her and get on to it.'

'Good,' said Macleod, 'I'll get our ill friend to bed and then I'm going to get some sleep myself. I'll see you at breakfast.'

Charming, thought Hope, *he's off to bed and muggins, who has been working her socks off, gets another job.* Waiting until Macleod and Mackintosh had left the room, Hope approached Jona and advised her of her plans for the evening and asked if she would tag along for the first part. There was a reluctance in her face but then Jona smiled and agreed but she did want to be back by eleven. That gave Hope three hours.

The women changed into more casual clothes and Hope let her hair out from her ponytail. Shimmering in every light it passed, Jona's hair transfixed Hope as its shininess was something she had never quite achieved. Unlike her own, which was inevitably tangled to some degree, Jona's was perfectly straight and Hope could feel the envy rising.

Hope left Jona sitting in the bar of Karen Gibbon's hotel while she walked the corridors to her room. Listening in, she heard an older woman and then someone middle-aged before the sound of a door opening. Hope raced off along the corridor, slowing to a steady walk when the door was properly opened. When footsteps sounded off in the opposite direction, she turned around and saw the rear of a woman in jeans and a raincoat.

Tailing the woman down to the bar, Hope saw her turn and take a drink from the barman and Hope slid herself in beside Jona. The woman was the same as the photograph Macleod had given her, Karen Gibbons. She seemed somewhat nervous and Hope whispered to Jona to simply look at Hope and talk away to her. Hope looked back at the pale Asian face and perfect hair but then looked beyond her to Karen Gibbons. The woman was glancing everywhere as she downed what looked like a neat gin.

Within a few minutes, she was on her feet and Hope tapped Jona's knee indicating she should follow. Outside, Hope watched Karen Gibbons curse the now-driving rain and open the door of a small three-door hatchback. Jumping into Jona's car, Hope had Jona tail the woman from as best a distance as possible on the narrow road which, while not a single track, was still difficult to negotiate in the dark. Occasionally, another car came the opposite direction and the lack of centre lines made passing more difficult for someone used to driving around Glasgow and Inverness. But Jona focused relentlessly and Hope believed they were not being seen as a following car.

Karen Gibbons drove out of Castlebay and along the west

side of Barra passing by Borve beach before making her way up to Allasdale. As they passed a sheep pen on their left-hand side, she pulled the car sharply into a passing place and Jona seemed to panic for a moment. Hope instructed her to drive on past and stop when instructed. The land around where Karen Gibbons had parked was flat and finding somewhere to stop so that it did not seem like they were watching her was not easy. Once they had rounded a corner, Hope had Jona pull off the road onto the grass verge and she scampered in the rain back along the road. Returning to the car moments later, she pulled a rucksack from the boot and told Jona to follow her.

Wishing her hair was tied up as it flung in a wet mess across her face, Hope realised that some sort of Kagool should have been in order but she was stuck with her leather jacket and felt the rivers of rain water running down her neck and across her front but she focused on the task ahead. Turning only once to make sure Jona was behind her, Hope sought out Karen Gibbons on the flat land ahead. She seemed to be making for the beach beyond the grass out to the west and had something in her hands, possibly a small spade or shovel. But what really interested Hope was the vehicle far beyond Karen's which had just switched off its headlights and was now sat in darkness by the roadside.

Rather than head directly to Karen Gibbons, Hope made her way in a parallel direction, keeping her spacing and could soon hear the crash of the sea above the driving rain. The wind was strong and her jacket blew out making her skin feel bitterly cold under the wet t-shirt. A glance at Jona saw her struggling behind and Hope gave her a hand. With one hand held against the rain, Jona started to make a faster pace and together the women managed a half run towards the beach where they knelt down in the sand. Hope pulled a pair of binoculars from her rucksack and stared off into the night.

There was no moonlight and she saw an image rather than Karen Gibbons, but the mix of black shadows showed a woman walking forward, apparently counting out steps. A hand was held out in front, maybe holding a compass, Hope thought, and the woman took a maze of steps until she decided she was in the right place. And then with great aplomb in the rain, she began to dig.

The area was just above the tideline but probably always clear of the sea. The woman was well built and she drove her spade into the ground in rapid succession, each time flinging an arm out to the sky. Beside Hope, Jona had a camera focused on Karen Gibbons and fired off repeated shots.

'Can you see her face?' asked Hope.

'Not really, it's very dark but I am getting something. Maybe they can enhance it back at the lab.'

Hope nodded and felt water running across her face, making her squint into the night. *Bloody Macleod, no wonder he wanted me out doing this while he was snug in bed.* A chill was starting across Hope's shoulders and she tried to wriggle to generate some heat.

'Baltic,' said Jona. 'I don't know why you have to put up with this nonsense; we have tents and everything.'

Grinning, Hope looked through the binoculars again but this time was scanning around the area. The car that had stopped was in her head, but she had not seen anyone around. That being said, it was dark and easy to miss people, especially if they were being furtive. Every murder so far had someone being attacked while by the sea. Maybe she should interrupt Karen Gibbons now, for her own safety. But then would they find out what she was looking for. The smart thing was to wait for her to dig up whatever she was looking for in case she did not find it and then they could remain undercover if she looked again. But she needed to hurry up and Hope was getting so very cold.

'Hope, do you see them?' asked Jona, pointing into the dark.

'No, where?'

'Maybe twenty feet from Karen Gibbons; she can't have noticed them—maybe it's the rain. They are moving towards her. Two of them.'

Hope was up on her feet and running now. As she looked ahead, she still saw only shadows and then a cry split the night. An image of a silhouette of a woman with a knife in her back, someone holding her tight from behind.

'Police! Halt, Police!'

'Run,' shouted a female voice. But the figure over Karen Gibbons, who had been deposited to the floor, was inside her coat looking for something. As Hope arrived, he stood up and she ducked low driving her shoulder at him, taking him off his feet. Together they rolled but as Hope broke off him, she felt a blow to the head and tumbled again. As she looked up to the sky, now prone on her back she saw a spade being lifted above her.

But then a fist connected with the spade bearer's jaw. 'Hell, that's sore,' said an Asian voice before she was hit by someone else.

'Come on, forget it,' said the voice again and Hope saw the two figures start to run off.

'Jona, see to Gibbons,' shouted Hope as she got unsteadily to her feet and turned to run after her attackers. 'And ring someone!'

A mix of sweat and rain stung her eyes, but Hope continued apace and began to gain on one of the figures. As they ran over the grass, she saw the first figure get into a car and start the engine. The second figure was only twenty feet from her, but she felt her lungs about to explode from the pressure put on them. The blow to the head was also starting to make her woozy and she felt her legs beginning to go. As the figure opened the car door, Hope came up from behind and made a desperate grab as the door shut. She grabbed the handle but the car drove off causing her to spin round and tumble to the ground. From her prone position she looked up and read the disappearing number plate.

Mobile, get your mobile out. Her hand felt inside her jacket and located it. She clicked the button at the side and saw three pictures at the bottom of the screen. One was Macleod, another Stewart and the last Ross. *Not Macleod, this needs to happen fast.* She pressed for Stewart.

'Stewart,' said a tired voice.

'Require assistance, Stewart. Allasdale on the road. Suspects departing in a car, northward. Request pursuit.'

'Colour, number plate, number of suspects,' said Stewart efficiently with no hint of panic in her voice.

Hope passed what she knew and then dragged herself to her feet. 'And an ambulance, Stewart, right away, suspect knifed and potentially in a life-threatening condition.' Again, there was no panic from the other end.

'I'm on it. I'll be with you shortly.'

Stumbling back to the beach, Hope realised that Jona and Karen Gibbons were out of sight. She dropped her jacket forming the arms into an arrow toward the beach. Then she ran through the rain, her top now totally sodden and her legs crying out from the spin they had received when the car departed. Hope arrived on the beach to see Jona desperately pumping Karen Gibbons' chest as she lay on the ground.

'Come on, dammit, come on. You're still there, still there.' Hope slid down beside Jona, but she waved her off and went back to working on the prone woman's chest. Karen Gibbons was spasming occasionally, but Hope thought that was the forceful compressions of Jona. Otherwise there seemed to be no life. The eyes were gazing nowhere and there seemed to be nothing else reacting to the forceful stimuli.

'Go to the road, get the ambulance,' cried Jona. 'You're no use to me here. Get them quick.'

Hauling herself back on her feet, Hope ran as hard as she could back to the road and then stood, her body fighting to stand large and tall in the weather as a marker for the ambulance. She put her leather coat back on but there was really little difference now. She was numb: whether this was the weather or the suspect fighting for her life that caused it, she could not tell.

The ambulance arrived, its blue lights lighting up the dark countryside and she flagged them down, yelling at them that it was a knifed woman on the beach, CPR in progress. Leading the ambulance crew down, she watched them jump in past Jona and take control, listening to Jona's brief situation report. Ten minutes later they called it.

Hope saw Jona fall to her knees, her top, face and body covered in blood, smearing into a thin liquid with the rain. Jona yelled out to the night and began to cry, sniffing loudly. Stepping up to her, Hope wrapped the woman up in a tight embrace. She wanted to say something, but what could you say. She knew the feeling; she knew they had done their best, but it still hurt more than most things in life.

Stewart arrived shortly afterwards and started taking control of the scene while Hope and Jona were shown to an ambulance where they were assessed before being put in the rear of a coastguard vehicle wrapped up in silver blankets and being given hot drinks. They did not speak and Jona sat in a kind of transfixed gaze, staring out to the darkness.

Macleod opened the door of the vehicle, wrapped in a large overcoat and looked at the pair of women huddling in the back. 'Don't beat yourselves up; you did all you could. But these guys are killers; she never stood a chance once they had knifed her. Nakamura, Mackintosh says she's going to handle this tonight, but she wants you ready in the morning, if you can manage that. And you can head back Hope after I get the detail of what happened from you.'

'She was digging, sir, but I don't know for what.'

'Whatever it is, it's important, as four people are now dead for it. We need to pick up the pace, Hope, or we won't have anyone left.'

'Are you sure Canna is connected?'

'Look,' said Macleod and pulled out a small piece of parchment. 'Inside Karen Gibbons' jacket. Stewart's going to the mainland tomorrow and we are going on the hunt here. There's too many dead, Hope. I'm just off with the Chief Inspector and she's talking about coming out here. How many of these treasure seekers are there out here? When does this end? Now we've got two pieces of the puzzle, so we need to get some answers. But tomorrow for you. I'll take your statement in a moment and then you two need to hit the sack. And that's an order.'

An hour later Hope stood in the shower, scrubbing off the

dirt and blood from the evening. Her body was still chilled but at least the room was warm, and she was starting to feel more alive. Part of her was thinking of checking on Jona who had not spoken on the trip back to the hotel, but she also did not want to wake her if she was asleep. Stepping out of the shower, Hope heard a knock on her door. Wrapping her gown around her, she opened it and found Jona standing there. Without invitation she stepped inside and then simply fell to the ground and began crying. Hope followed her to the floor and wrapped her up. 'It's okay, girl; I'm here for you—it's okay.'

Chapter 11

Macleod sat behind a desk in the local station and watched Mackintosh enter the office. He knew there were a number of reporters outside and she would have to run the gauntlet in coming to him and after such a night, he hoped she had the wisdom to simply keep her head down and keep walking. The local coastguard and fire service were helping out in protecting the scene, but he needed more officers and had told his boss. In fairness to her, they would be on the next ferry but at the moment, he was very stretched.

'Here,' said Macleod, standing as Mackintosh entered the room and then pulling out a seat for her. The woman flopped into the chair and then noticed the cup of coffee before her. 'Yes, that's for you, Hazel. You deserve it, coming out after your news and that.'

'I'm the boss, Seoras, like yourself. You wouldn't run and hide either, would you?'

The veneer of steely grit might have impressed anyone who had not seen her fall apart at her onerous news of cancer, but Macleod was not buying it. But if that's how she needed to present herself until she left the island then he would let her. 'So, what do we know?'

'Knifed from behind, very neatly in terms of a fast death but there was a lot of blood. Jona had no chance of saving her, poor girl. She's fairly new, you know, good on the science but this side of it must have been a shock to her. At least the Canna body was already cold, but to have someone clinging to life in your hands—it's not an experience I would wish on anyone.'

'Have you lost someone?' asked Macleod, sipping on his coffee.

'Two. One a motorbike accident I was driving past and the other a stab victim. Just me for twenty minutes. Seoras, I can still see her. But I have two successes to weigh up against these deaths, Jona does not. Take it easy on her. I know you'll need her a lot over these coming days and I think she's more than up to it, but don't give her any of that bullish attitude of yours. And none of the weak woman crap either.'

Macleod looked offended. 'I treat you all with respect and as for my female colleagues, I hope I treat you equally.'

'You try, Seoras, I know you try. But it can't be easy. I mean, working with McGrath, she'd turn any man's head.'

'That's unfair,' he snapped and then felt bad for snarling at Mackintosh.

'No, it's not. You turn my head and I have to try and moderate myself. Why's it any different for you? But sometimes you see us as fragile and then it pops out, that protective streak. It's endearing to some of us but it won't be to Jona. It isn't to McGrath either. You need to let her fly.'

'I've brought Hope on, pushed her to go for Sergeant,' Macleod defended himself, 'and yes, it would be easier to work on a male team, it would. But they deserve their place, McGrath and Stewart, on their own merit. As do you.'

'Soft soap me,' laughed Mackintosh but then looked at him endearingly, her eyes hinting at tears. 'Thanks for yesterday, for being there. I know it can't be easy what with your Jane. Don't feel guilty; you were a rock in a storm for me. God knows how I'll get through the next part.'

'When's the treatment start?'

'Two days in Glasgow.'

'You got anyone there.' Mackintosh shook her head in a pitiful negative. 'Then Jane will go down with you. I need to tell her anyway, in case anyone starts a rumour about us, make sure she understands.'

Mackintosh reached forward and touched Macleod's hand. 'Thank you.'

Macleod nodded and then removed himself to the rear of his desk. 'Anything else to tell me? We got a little bit unprofessional there.'

'No, you didn't. As I said, she was knifed skillfully, dying if not immediately then in quick fashion. I can't find anything from them at the scene yet, but we are still looking. The car you heard about. Burnt out and again that's something we are working on. You have the copies of the parchment, which looks to be very standard paper, but I am having it sent to the lab for analysis. The first map at Canna was made on basic parchment, untraceable really, and with a basic ink pen. Again, getting us nowhere.'

'There seems to be little forensically,' said Macleod, 'so I hope we can do a little ferreting on the mainland—discover something. I still don't understand why there's a murder on Canna, but the maps show they are connected.'

'Did you hear what the press are calling the murders? The Pirate Club. People digging on the beach, rather apt.'

There was a rap at the door and Hope entered with Jona trailing behind. Macleod saw the lack of sleep in both their faces but Jona looked like she had seen a ghost, her skin even paler than normal. Mackintosh got to her feet and embraced the woman like she was her mother. It was not the professional attitude Macleod had desired but given the circumstances, he understood why. Hope stood to one side and he simply nodded at her and she nodded back. She was good to go.

'There's another room through there if you two want to do a handover and then it's back to work, Miss Nakamura,' said Macleod and Mackintosh looked at him. 'I'll have a word before you go, Hazel.' It just slipped out and he understood what she had said. *Hazel*. Not Mackintosh. A softer tone—well, at least she found it endearing.

The forensic team left and Hope took the seat in front of the desk. Swinging a leg of her jeans across the other she seemed agitated.

'How was last night?' asked Macleod.

'You got my statement.'

'I meant Jona; how was she?'

'Not good. Don't tell anyone but she spent the night in my room.' Macleod's eyes raised. 'Hell, Seoras, do you see everything in that way? I swear that's an island thing. In case you are wondering she's not inclined to women and she simply needed someone to hold her, if you can understand that. Anyway, where's Mackintosh off to?'

'Hospital, medical issue,' said Macleod, flatly. *And yes, I can understand that.*

'So, it's on Jona. I'd keep an eye on her, Seoras; she's struggling.'

'You do that for me, Hope. You seem to have a rapport.' *She's female and Asian, not doubt I'll manage to cause offence at some point. Especially if the old instincts kick in.* 'Stewart's on the first

97

flight out, off tailing leads. We need to mount a search here for our two runaways from last night, so I want you to organise that but as we are still struggling for officers make sure we don't endanger anyone, these runaways are killers. Everything at a distance, observation only is the watchword for any of the other services.'

Macleod pulled the copy of the map Mackintosh had sent him and placed it on the table before rooting in a drawer and placing another copy of a map beside it. Then he took a copy of an Ordnance Survey map of the area and placed it on the table.

'Two pieces of map, Hope, and people looking for something, prepared to kill to get it. I am bringing in Karen Gibbons' mother to talk to us, but she was in bed asleep last night so I though it better to let her sleep and they can advise her in the morning about her daughter's death. We'll need her in some sort of state and I thought the fatigue of being woken up in the night and the shock of the news might not be a good combination.'

'True,' said Hope. 'Is Stewart looking into their background any further?'

'Karen Gibbons seems clean, but I have tasked Stewart with connecting the dots between our victims. In the meantime, we have a manhunt here and that's your baby.'

Hope looked at the maps and tried to see the connection between them. 'Why are the maps basically blank except for a few dots, Seoras? I mean, if you read the text on the back it tells you what the dots are and then gives a referencing co-ordinate off of *Dusty's Harbour*. Where is that? What is it?'

'I reckon you need it to solve the puzzle which is why people are looking for the other pieces. Yes, there's a reference on each map but this referencing co-ordinate seems critical. I tried this morning using lots of harbours as references but all I got was lots of points which I could look at although none were on a beach. Given that they all seem to be looking on the coast I didn't want to start digging up twenty-plus locations. We don't even know what they are looking for.'

'Given that our murderers appear to be young, we can assume it's something recent, perhaps?'

'No,' said Macleod. 'Everyone else is older so that means the young people might just be following up on something older. I know we're clutching at straws at the moment but ruling things out too soon will hurt us, Hope.'

As he spoke, his mobile began vibrating and Macleod picked it up. 'Macleod.'

'Stewart, sir. I'm about to go for the plane but I thought you would want to know this right away. I was researching our victims and I have started onto their immediate families. Our Vatersay victim, Alasdair MacPhail, has no previous record but his wife does, or at least has some sort connection with crime.'

'Explain.'

'Well, I called the team I used to work with in Glasgow to see if there was any background on MacPhail but one of the lads there is from Newcastle and transferred up five years ago. He recalls working on a case and there was a MacPhail they could not pin a theft down on. As he recalls, it was a piece of artwork, but she had an alibi. Although it seemed fabricated, they could not prove it. Long story short, sir, is that she has form and I want to go and dig up more about her. So, I'd like to head to Newcastle if that's okay with you.'

Macleod breathed in deeply, thinking to himself. This

was a change in that Stewart was now going after suspected felons rather than families of victims and he was weary of her snooping around territory they did not know. 'I'll get in touch with Newcastle and see if they can help, and to let them know you are in the area. But tread carefully, Stewart, we have bodies mounting here and I doubt they will go easy on a snooper even if we are the police. I'm sending Ross to work with you, cover your back sort of thing. No risks, Kirsten; if something is sticky, talk to Newcastle and get backup.'

'Yes, sir,' said an excited voice on the other end of the line. 'It's getting close to check-in time. I have to go but thank you.'

Macleod wondered if he were playing this right, but he knew the girl could dig things up and Ross should be able to curb any overenthusiasm that could lead to unsafe situations. He briefed Hope on the conversation and then dismissed her.

As he sat back, cup in his hand, staring at the maps before him, the door opened again and Mackintosh walked in.

'How's Jona?'

'She'll be okay. Shaken but I think she's found a friend in McGrath. Hasn't stopped talking about her. But I came through to say goodbye, Seoras. I need to catch the plane.'

'Stewart's going too if you need company.'

'She's ahead of you, picking me up in a moment; otherwise, you'd offer to take me, and you have enough on.'

'I'll get Jane to meet you at Inverness today.'

'You don't need to, really. I'll be okay.'

Macleod took Mackintosh's hands. 'I know you will and you'll fight like a wild one against this, but no one should walk along these paths alone. Jane will want to help, she's like that. Same way you would for someone else.'

Mackintosh leaned forward and hugged Macleod tightly.

'Thank you, Seoras. You're a man of faith, so pray for me, pray damn hard.'

With that, she broke the embrace and turned without looking back out of the door, but he could hear the sniff pulling the emotion back inside. He collapsed into his chair, feeling the tug inside that made him think this could be a last time seeing her. As much as she had chased after him, a taken man, he could not help but like her. Determined woman, so like Jane.

The door flew open and Hope stood before him looking a little flustered. 'Sir, we just lost our lead. Gibbons' mother, she's dead.'

'Dead?'

'She woke up and started demanding to know where her daughter was. When they told her, she collapsed. Just died, sir, just died.'

Macleod grabbed his coffee cup and threw it against the wall smashing it into tiny pieces, the liquid spraying the wall. Hope looked at him, in shock.

'What? Every damn lead, Hope, every damn lead!'

Chapter 12

She looks like a ghost, still, thought Macleod. He did not know Jona Nakamura well but the girl had obviously had a rough time over the last twenty-four hours. Yet she was still here and working. Sitting before him in the Castlebay station, Jona was confirming that the older Gibbons—for Karen Gibbons had not gone with her father's name but rather her mother's—had indeed died from a massive heart attack probably brought on by the news of the death of her daughter.

'Every time we get somewhere, it gets snatched away,' said Macleod under his breath.

'I don't know if we can gain anything else from her. We are searching the room and taking prints and whatever we can find. There are addresses in various formats for the pair of them but according to DS McGrath, they don't check out. I have sent DNA samples away from the incident last night and the lab is proceeding with those as fast as they can. I'll let you know if anything significant comes back.'

Macleod stood up and paced the room, looking around wildly as he thought. When he stopped for a moment, he realised that Jona was still there, obviously waiting for him to say she could go. He looked at her for a moment and once again saw her covered in blood, her face a mess of tears and sweat, crushed at not saving a life before her. Now she was in a smart jacket and blouse with a pair of dark trousers, but her face still showed the scars.

'Good, Jona, you're doing good. Look, this case has a bucket of attention coming with it and you've lost your cover but just do your job, nothing more, nothing less. I realise you are struggling with last night so if you need to release let me know. I can help.' Macleod was not actually sure he could.

'Hope, I mean, DS McGrath has been immensely helpful, sir, but I understand. To be honest I need to just bury this until we get finished. I'm sure you understand that.'

Only too well, thought Macleod, *but it's not healthy*. 'Just make sure you take time to deal with it when you can. Don't let things linger in the background because they don't leave. As for the press and any other pressure from above, that's mine, not yours, to deal with. You worry about what I need from you and that's all. I have big shoulders.'

'But no coffee cups I heard.'

There was a silence as Macleod struggled to take in the joke. His mind raced through whether this was an attack, a friendly jibe, or what. His staff did not normally throw in such quips, even Mackintosh came at him from a completely different angle. 'No,' he said and forced a smile. 'Don't be up too late, Jona; you need your rest.'

When she had left, Macleod flopped into his chair again and thought through where the day had left him. It was nine o'clock already and the Chief Inspector had been in conference with him for an hour on top of the press conference, leaving him exhausted. Stewart had called and was in a hotel in Glasgow, ready to start out first thing in the morning. No doubt she would be running through files on her laptop, checking wild links just in case they brought something up.

The island had been combed that day by a helicopter and search teams, looking for the pair who killed Karen Gibbons but there was no sign of them. Whoever they were, they were no mugs. Barra was not the largest island at around four miles across and they had brought in teams from the other services from the other isles, up as far as Stornoway. But all the searching had been fruitless.

Macleod remained, studying reports until around midnight and then headed for his hotel. Calmly walking through the small scrum of reporters, he held up a hand for no comment and forced a smile as they asked questions on the hoof. A newly arrived officer kept them back at the entrance to the hotel and Macleod let his mask drop. As he entered the lobby, he heard a strong shower begin and was thankful he had missed a soaking, deciding he had two things to do before he slept. A quick call to Jane discovered she was travelling down to Glasgow with Mackintosh the next day and that she had experienced a rough day with the woman. But there was no complaint from her, just concern for him.

And as his last duty for the night, he rapped on Hope's door. Hope asked who it was.

'Macleod.'

'Come in.'

He swung the door open and saw Hope cross legged on the floor with Jona sitting beside her in the same pose. Both sat in pyjamas with their eyes closed. For a moment Macleod did not know where to look as Hope's informality caught him out again. Neither woman was indecent, but Macleod felt that old standard from his upbringing of a woman not being seen in her

104

bedclothes by anyone but her husband. Today this standard had been tossed to the wind and surely Hope and Jona would think him mad to be embarrassed but he still did feel it, that touch of shame and even naughtiness. *Grow up Seoras, come on.*

After a minute of silence, Hope uncrossed her legs and stood up. Behind her, Jona unfolded herself, put her dressing gown on and then gave Hope a brief hug. With a quick 'Sir', Jona left the room and Hope sat down on her bed directing Macleod to a chair by the dressing table.

'She okay?'

'No, but she's getting there. Are you okay? You look beat.'

'Weight of the world, McGrath. Search continuing tomorrow then. You got everyone you need.'

'No,' said Hope flatly 'but we have got who we can get so it'll have to do.'

'Okay. I just wanted to see you were okay. You were a bit annoyed at me bringing you here. You understand why? Stewart's investigations are useful, but this is where the focus of the press and the force will be. I need someone experienced to handle the day to day.'

'I know, Seoras but don't expect me not to be pissed. I was running my own investigation, and it felt good if scary. But you won't get complaints from me—you have enough, and Mackintosh is worrying you. You're actually fond of her despite how you protest about her. Don't make that face—it's not obvious to everyone. I just know you well.' Macleod felt his face going red. 'Get to bed, Seoras, busy day tomorrow.'

At three o'clock in the morning, Macleod wandered downstairs to the hotel lobby unable to sleep. He had thought about having a quick walk but one of the heavy showers had come on, so he simply sat in a chair and looked out of the window into the dark vista beyond. Trying to calm his mind, he felt himself drift but then he was seeing Jane's face; she was beside Mackintosh. And then Ross was asking him why they were staying at this house. Then Jona started saying his fingerprints were over them both. And then Hope placed handcuffs on him.

Waking with a start, Macleod saw the same dark vista his eyes had closed to.

'Can't sleep. Me neither.' He saw Hope in a chair across from him, dressed in a leather jacket and her pyjamas. 'I was going to take the air but it's pissing down out there.'

Macleod gave a faint smile and nodded. As he went to speak, Hope's mobile vibrated. He looked away as she picked it up, but he was keen to know who was calling at three in the morning, it was not her boyfriend Allinson's way. Hope jumped from her seat, still on the call. Throwing her hand over the mouthpiece she said, 'Person on Vatersay with a spade. Get the car.'

Macleod walked into the pouring rain and sought out his vehicle. Once inside he started the engine and brought the car to the front of the hotel where Hope jumped in, now dressed in a t-shirt and jeans, covered by the same leather jacket. The headlights lit up the narrow street out of Castlebay and he swung the car hard left onto the road to Vatersay. It was a matter of minutes before they crossed the causeway at Caolas and raced along the coastal road to Traigh Siar where Alasdair MacPhail had been murdered.

As they got close, Macleod saw a police car through the driving rain parked off the road beside another vehicle. Pulling up, Macleod saw an officer beside the car who waved him over.

'Suspect on the beach, sir. I have asked for more units. It's a single male, approximately thirty years old and has a green anorak on. He's got a metal detector and a rucksack with him. Hunt is over at the edge of the beach watching him.'

Macleod nodded and ran over to the second officer who was lying down at the top of the hillock that led down to the beach. Getting down beside the man, Macleod took a pair of binoculars from him and studied the suspect on the beach carefully. The man's hood had fallen down and a black-haired face looked weather beaten and tired but there was a smile on the man's face. A metal detector showed a green light and was set aside as a small spade was taken from the rucksack and the sand was dug up in a frantic fashion.

'Hope, get round the other side of him in case he makes a run for it, although he doesn't look like a man in shape to make a run.' Hope moved off and Macleod watched the man continue to dig. Behind him, he started to hear vehicles arriving and he told Constable Hunt to go and make sure no one disturbed the man's actions with a cavalcade of noise from the road.

It took the man half an hour of digging before he was standing inside a hole up to his knees, digging harder than ever. Occasionally he would bring the metal detector into the hole and then give a nod as the light showed green again. Suddenly, the man bent over and pulled something up from the sand. Macleod got to his feet and motioned Hope to start moving in.

But the man did not see them and simply climbed out of the hole and walked towards the sea where he dipped the item into the water before shaking it dry. This seemed a futile effort given that the rain had not abated, and the man turned around almost walking into Macleod. Hope flanked him and the man looked bemused.

107

'Can I help you?' he asked in a worried voice.

'DI Macleod, sir, and that is DS McGrath. What are you doing?'

'Hunting.' The man saw Macleod's confused face. 'I'm detecting, looking for the treasure. The papers said it was a Pirate Club that was causing all the murders so there must be treasure if there's pirates. And I was right, look.' The man held out a hand clutching a golden cross. 'Amazing isn't it?'

'What's your name, sir?' asked Macleod.

'David, David Hobart. I came over yesterday and thought I'd look here since your people were finished. And I was right. Look at that beauty. How much do you think it's worth?'

'Mr Hobart, I think we need a chat, but somewhere less wet. If you can accompany us and bring your gear with you. If you'll give the cross to DS McGrath, she'll look after it for you.'

'Okay, but that's mine, all right; I found it. You saw me find it, right? So, it's mine.'

'I did see you find it, sir, but as to who owns it, I think we'll wait until investigations show us what it is. Now, hurry up. I'm soaked in this rain.'

Back at the Castlebay station, Macleod found a towel and dried himself down as best he could before joining David Hobert in the tight room that was serving as his office. In the corner, the man's rucksack and metal detector sat, dripping water onto the floor. The man still wore his anorak. Hope was standing behind Macleod's desk as there were only two seats. Macleod waved the seat at Hope and she leaned close to him to whisper, 'Hardly, you're the boss.' He was only trying to be chivalrous.

'Better out of that rain, Mr Hobart, I think,' said Macleod and gratefully lifted a cup of coffee that was on his desk. After taking a gulp, Macleod continued, 'Now from the top, sir, can you tell me exactly what you were doing in the middle of the night on the beach at Vatersay?'

'Well, officer, it's like this. I am a hunter of treasure. I spend most weekends when I'm not having to stop on at the Revenue, combing likely areas for things that are buried. I take that baby everywhere,' said the man, looking over endearingly at his detector in the corner.

'The Revenue?' asked Macleod. 'You're a civil servant?'

'Yes, have been for twenty years. You can check with them, been a model employee, or just about for that time. But I like to get out and about and have been detecting for the last ten years since my divorce. Gives me something to do and I get to see the world. And at odd times of the year. Take up here, for example; most people only come up in the summer months, or maybe spring, but here's me in winter. Different place I suspect.'

'And you came up here to do your detecting?' said Hope. 'Why here, specifically?'

'As I said on the beach, following the Pirate Club. It's big news. Can I get into my bag and show you? I mean don't shoot me or anything, I'm just getting the paper.'

Macleod saw Hope smile at the man as she clarified, 'We rarely shoot anyone, Mr Hobart.'

It took a hunt of thirty seconds before the man joyfully pulled out a creased newspaper and brought it over to the table. Flopping it down before Macleod, he spun it around so Macleod could read it and opened at the inside pages. There was a large spread talking about the murders and giving photographs of various sites and of officers standing by crime scenes. Then there was a photograph of the Vatersay victim,

Alasdair MacPhail, standing with a MOD medal, looking as proud as punch.

'He's why I'm up here. Brilliant singer, officer, just brilliant. I have some of his recordings and when I saw he had died I was actually a bit upset. Beside myself really because I felt like I knew the man. Never met him but music can do that to you, don't you think?'

Macleod did not think so but smiled back. 'If you say so, Mr Hobart, and it's Inspector Macleod and that's Sergeant McGrath.'

'Oh, sorry. Important then. Well, you would be with these many deaths. Well, I saw the paper saying MacPhail had died and then I saw the front cover.' The man flicked the paper back to the front and Macleod saw a picture of himself standing on Vatersay. An Admiral's uniform had been super imposed on him and there was a map of Barra and Canna with large black crosses where the bodies had been found. A title read, 'The Pirate Club'.

Shaking his head, Macleod tried not to fume. He glanced at the banner at the head of the paper and realised it was one of the crasser tabloids. He scanned the rest of the paper finding that news of the incidents ran for seven pages. There was a photograph of Mackintosh in her white coverall suit and for a moment, he caught himself thinking about her trip to Glasgow. But then a picture of Hope and Jona Nakamura on page four caught his eye. She was described as 'the stunning new Sergeant', and 'her forensic beauty'. Hope looked down over his shoulder and he could feel her smile building. The only words accompanying himself were haggard and grizzly. It really was the stuff of the gutter.

'Why Vatersay, Mr Hobart? Why not Canna?'

'Well, Alasdair MacPhail was a clever bloke and I have no idea who that woman was on Canna. And then there seems to be more happening here so I reckoned it would be a better chance for the gold, or whatever treasure they were hiding.'

'But why treasure?' asked Hope. 'Why not a feud?'

'Pirate Club, Sergeant, says so right there,' and the man pointed to the headline. 'And then inside,' he continued, sweeping the pages to page four where he pointed to the paragraph under Hope's picture. 'Macleod's bracing first officer and her oriental colleague left the island having recovered no loot which focuses the investigation on the Isle of Barra where the loot is suspected to be hidden deep beneath the sand. With the attention of these stunning deckhands, the battle-weary Macleod faces a race to find the plunder before more bodies litter the beaches.'

'And you came because of this?' said Macleod, struggling to keep his temper in check.

'Absolutely, Inspector, I reckon there's more out there too. I mean the paper's right, isn't it? I found the cross. Stuff of legend—sort of thing you would find in a pirate haul.'

Macleod had to admit when painted in that light, it did indeed cast a romantic and teasing view. But people had died, and this was no fairy tale. 'Have you ever seen the cross before, Mr Hobart.'

The man shook his head. 'Have no idea what it's worth. But I found it; you wrote that down somewhere, didn't you? I mean if it's worth a lot, it's mine.'

'People other than I will establish ownership if the item is indeed a find. At the moment it is part of a murder investigation, Mr Hobart, so do not expect to see it very soon. We'll be checking your details out in the morning so don't leave the island and kindly keep off the crime scenes.'

The man was escorted out leaving his paper for Macleod, advising him that the journalists were onto something. Sitting back in his chair, Macleod pointed Hope to the now-free-one opposite and watched her collapse into it. She smiled, almost giggling to herself.

'It's all right for you,' said Macleod, 'Bracing, stunning. I get haggard, grizzly, battle weary.'

'Do you think they might actually have something? I mean, that did look like a significant piece of antique gold.'

'Who knows where the cross is from? That's Miss Naka-mura's job to tell us. But they are searching for something and not afraid to kill for it. And let's get them before we have any more deaths, or we'll look like some sad show with the haggard Inspector and your bracing self with her stunning sidekick. Not an image we want.'

'No, it's not,' said Hope suddenly. 'Allinson won't like it either.'

No, he will not, thought Macleod seeing Hope's partner in his mind. *Jane will just laugh at my description.*

Chapter 13

Kirsten Stewart stood in front of the Newcastle tenement and fought to keep her frustration under control. Last night, her brother's carer had rung to advise he had been edgy all day and that it would be good if she could swing by to see if Kirsten could calm him down. The change of scenery and people from Stornoway to Inverness had not been one that he had appreciated but she had hoped he would settle down after a few months. But little had changed and although she tried to hide it from her everyday work, it was starting to become a burden she carried everywhere.

Before her stood a three-story reddish brick building that housed many flats. It ran as one building along the entire street but was like a tower block tilted onto its side in that there was at least one family in each floor of each longitudinal section. The area was reasonably upmarket and Stewart wondered why the flats were so sought after. There was plenty of nightlife around but for her the city was crowded and noisy. Even in Inverness she had chosen to live on one of the many satellite villages surrounding it.

The address she held in her hand was for Alasdair MacPhail but the Newcastle constable who visited the apartment to announce the news of his demise had found the flat to be empty. Further records had found that he had been widowed three months previous. But there was little else to go on, so Stewart had dragged Ross from his bed at six o'clock that morning to find her connection to the case, wherever it lay in Newcastle.

Inside the tenement, Stewart found a stone staircase leading up to the top floor and the door of MacPhail's flat. It was glass fronted, albeit frosted, and she stood looking in as best she could. But the glass meant that everything was blurry. A brown carpet inside warped into a confusion for its pattern but she saw enough to see that it was undisturbed, nothing sitting on top of it. Reaching for the letterbox, Kirsten found it stiff and it took two attempts to open it. Pushing back the black brush interior of the opening, she realised that there was nothing out of place, like the hallway had not been touched in recent times.

Footsteps behind her made her turn but it was Ross arriving from the floor below. 'Neighbours say they haven't seen anyone here for at least three months, not since his wife passed on. Apparently, he wasn't seen much in there anyway.'

'Do you think that this flat has been quiet these last months, Ross? I mean, just no one in here. The hallway is immaculate but there's no post. If MacPhail was away there should be post.'

'So, someone's been in.'

'Maybe, but what else do you do if going away, especially if it's for a long time. I think we need to check the post office and see if there's a re-direct on this.'

Ross nodded and they descended the stairs back to the car where Stewart googled the local post office number. Ten minutes later they were heading for an address on the opposite side of Newcastle and into a more salubrious area.

The house was a newly built two-storey, but it had pillars either side of a green door and looked like something from a show-house catalogue. There were pots with perfectly budding plants along the drive and hanging baskets were on the outside walls. The small garden had stunning colours and Stewart wondered where someone would get the time to produce all of this. As they walked up the drive, a woman emerged from the rear of the house holding a pair of garden clippers like they were a weapon.

'Who are you?' she snarled.

'DCs Stewart and Ross, ma'am. We'd like to ask you about a Mr Alasdair MacPhail. Are you aware of the name?'

'Aye,' she replied, her Glasgow accent coming to the fore. 'I know him, or knew him. Dead up at Barra.'

'Did you know him well?' asked Ross.

'Well, for the last ten years I was keeping the smile on his face at night so I would say I knew him as well as anyone—probably better than that sour-faced cow they called his wife. Finally got her out of our life and he has to go and pop his clogs.'

'Forgive me, Ma'am, but you don't seem all that sad that he's gone.'

'I'm not. Ally was okay, treated me well, enjoyed our fun and asked for nothing much in return except to look after his bairns. But they grew into big bairns and then a load of arrogant wee shits. Well rid of them, hated them. Especially the eldest, right bastard.'

Stewart was aware that the conversation was loud and there might be some neighbours listening in despite how spaced out the new estate was. 'Should we go inside to discuss this?' asked Stewart.

'Why? Do you want a cup of tea because I am making

nothing? I don't care who knows. I'm better off without them. Cleared out when their mother died, bitching about getting what was due them. She never gave Ally anything from when she died but instead it went to the bairns. Well, they went on about taking what was theirs, something their mother had kept. I didn't ask because she was part of a nasty firm. She might have been older now but in her day, she was up to no good. I can't believe he married her.'

'What sort of stuff was she in to?' Ross asked.

'They reckon she had goods stashed away. Ally said that to me once when I complained that he would still go and see her. And not socially either, I knew he was bedding us both. But he told me she had a load of cash somewhere, a big score from past days. Fairy tales, that was a problem with Ally, his damn fairy tales. But I've had it up to here with them. That's what took him to Barra.'

'Wait a minute,' Stewart said holding up a hand. 'He went to Barra looking for some sort of contraband from his wife's previous scores. We know she was a thief but we don't know what she stole.'

'No, you don't. Neither do I, as I didn't want to have anything come back at me, but Ally said there was enough for us to clear off to the Bahamas for the rest of our existence. Now he's dead chasing his dream. That's why I didn't ask, didn't want that for myself. No, he was a good man on your arm but thick as they come sometimes. Still I got this house from him and that'll do me until I go his way.'

'What's your name?' asked Stewart.

'Maureen Ghillies and I have told you nothing you couldn't work out for yourselves so that's all you're getting. I don't want dragged in. So be off with you; I got gardening to do.'

Ross glanced at Stewart looking for her call as for what to do now. Although they held the same rank, Ross had held it for longer and normally would take the senior role between the pair of them. But Stewart was pushing the leads they were following so Ross had acquiesced and now simply waited for a response. This left Stewart flapping a little, but she held her poise. If you stood silent but purposeful, they usually reckoned you were sizing them out and not scrambling to know what the heck to do.

'I'll level with you, Mrs Ghillies,' said Stewart. 'We don't have a lot of leads to chase and you have just indicated that Mr MacPhail's children may be partaking in whatever is causing all these deaths so as much as you want to remain out of the loop and not get involved, if there are no other leads, then we have to pursue this one to the hilt. We'll get a warrant and you'll need to come downtown and help us with enquiries. Or you can give me the whole story. I'll be satisfied and then you and I can never see each other again.'

Maureen looked at Stewart sharply and then nodded to her to follow her to the rear of the house. The back garden was another model of horticultural excellence and Stewart found herself being offered a seat at a cast-iron table.

'I'm still making no tea,' said the woman in a hushed tone. 'What do you need to know?'

'According to my records—and all I have is a number—Mr MacPhail had three children by his late wife.'

'That's correct, two girls and a boy. Andy's the lad, twenty and fairly strong. Cheryl's the older girl, a year younger than Andy and quite astute whereas Andy's more violent. And then there's Debbie, seventeen and a vixen with it. Not afraid to mess about with the boys' emotions but also not afraid to hurt

117

when she wants to. She kicked the face off a guy who tried to make her go where she didn't want to. Like her mother and she's got a brain up there too.'

'Do you have any photographs?' asked Ross.

Maureen nodded and then disappeared into the house before bringing back a newspaper. It was a local magazine, printed to have a small circulation and Stewart saw the price of £1.99 on its cover. The cover also had a splash photograph of Alasdair MacPhail, his wife, and three youths.

'That's from the local music society rag; there were quite a number produced, maybe two hundred so they can't trace that picture to me. There's a piece inside about Ally's music. Debbie's the one showing the cleavage; wee vixen like I said.'

'Thank you,' said Stewart. 'When they disappeared after their mother's death, did she leave them anything special that you saw? I mean, they went racing off to look for something, some former contraband, so did she give them anything to help in that regard.'

'It must have been a map picture that was on the wall of her house. I know this because Ally had a photograph of it on his mobile and he studied it sometimes in the middle of the night asking, "Where are you?" Told him I'm right here but he was miles away.'

'Where did she have it in her house?'

'No idea, and that's your lot. I've told you what I know and that's all you're getting.'

'One last question?' said Stewart holding a hand up. 'Do you have any addresses for these kids?'

The woman laughed. 'No and I don't want any addresses. They can just sod off. I helped raise them and all they gave me was scorn. I was like a stepmother but I wasn't good enough, not like their mother who abandoned them. So as far as I'm concerned, they can take a boat down the creek and I wouldn't hand them a paddle. Let them drift downriver and keep going until they go over the falls. Goodbye, detectives; you know the way out.'

Tucking the magazine with the picture of MacPhail's family away, Stewart nodded at Ross to leave. Back in the car, Ross drove them to the services off the main road that runs around Newcastle, skirting Gateshead before passing Newcastle itself and heading further north. He filled the car with petrol and then came back with two coffees which he handed to Stewart. Instead of driving off, he took the car to a car park beside the petrol station and parked up.

'What's the plan of action?' he asked to a deep-in-thought Stewart.

'We send the picture to the boss along with what we have learnt. And then we go to our friends here in Newcastle. McPhail's wife was a con and she had part of the map. There's been other maps too, so I reckon there's a crew who all have these pieces. We need to go into her past and find the crew. These kids are on the lookout for them too and they seemed prepared to kill.'

'You reckon they committed the murders?'

'It's a good hypothesis. Of course, it could be a free for all. But we'll see our Geordie friends and give them the names of our characters, including Karen Gibbons, our old man who's running around, and some photos of our Canna victim. I think the action's going to happen up there, but the answers are down here in Newcastle.'

Ross drove to the main police station in Newcastle where the pair introduced themselves and requested the help of the local unit. Together, in the company of a young constable named Stavely, they trawled the records for the history of Alasdair Macleod's wife, picking up a multitude of names and addresses for further investigation. By late afternoon Stewart had organised a tour of possible addresses for former known associates and acquaintances.

The first stop was at an out-of-town estate where the first house they came across had windows boarded up and a front door with the glass smashed in. A shopping trolley was in the front lawn and Stewart wondered if they would find anything inside. When Ross pushed back the open door, she could smell faeces and urine. The stench nearly overcame her and she held her breath as she continued inside the house. The living room sported a sofa with mould all over it and the walls were white with a fungus. Clearly the rain had been coming through the roof and causing an unstoppable tide of decay. On the floor was a rolled-up sleeping bag and when Ross shouted from the kitchen, Stewart ran through. On the floor was a sleeping man, wrapped up in a jacket and with an empty bottle of vodka beside him.

'Dead end,' said Ross. 'He looks like nobody I saw in the photos of her associates. What do you think?'

'You're right. Let's get a move on before I lose all sense of smell. Poor bugger living like this.'

As Stewart stepped back out of the house, she saw a girl standing by their car. She was just over five feet tall with greasy black hair and a tight crop top on and black boots and skin-tight leggings. As she glanced over at Stewart, the girl stared, her large, round earrings dangling almost level with her chin. Although at a distance, Stewart could see the abundance of make-up on the girl's face and she placed her in her late teens.

Turning to Ross, she asked, 'Do you see that girl by the car?'

Ross stepped out of the house and looked up. 'No. Why?'

'She's just there . . .' Stewart saw their car now standing on its own and the girl nowhere in sight. She must have moved quickly. 'There was a girl there, Ross, late teens but looking like a real tart. She was watching us. Could have sworn she was.'

As they reached the car, Ross pointed to the rear door on the passenger side. The legend 'Pigs' was scrawled on the door, possibly with a key or something else sharp. 'Sweet place,' said Ross, 'I hope your list has more upmarket places from here on in.'

But Stewart tried to think of the face she had seen. It was at a distance, but something was bothering her, like she knew the face from somewhere. But it had only been a brief look from afar and she was unable to pull the feeling from her head and put it into a real context. 'Next stop, Ross, let's go.'

Chapter 14

Hope pulled her leather jacket around her shoulders and left her hotel room, walking the corridors back to the main lobby and bar area. The searching of Barra for their two suspects had proved fruitless and even Mr Dickerson or Drummer, or whatever he was called, was proving elusive. Stewart was searching for more leads on the mainland and Hope wished she were there and not on Barra where she felt Macleod was using her in a not-so-helpful way.

Stewart or Ross could organise the manhunt; after all, it did not involve the ingenuity that uncovering the true background of this case required. How had she gone from being in charge of her own case to effectively holding the boss's hand? The other angle was where was Dusty's Harbour? If they could find it, they might be able to trace the location of more items from the maps but at the moment they had no idea who Dusty was. Night had fallen and Stewart had sent word about finding MacPhail's partner and about his children being on the hunt for what was theirs.

Hope walked to the small community hall where Jona Nakamura had continued the work her boss had started before disappearing on the plane. It was all very secretive, and Hope wondered just what was going on with Macleod and

Mackintosh, but the woman had seemed far from herself. Still, it had given a great opportunity to Jona to prove herself and despite her horror at the incident on the beach, she was throwing herself into the work.

The hour was past eleven when Hope entered the community hall and nodded to the single police officer at the door. Most of the evidence was sitting around in bags and overnight there would be protection around it. Sitting in a small room off the main hall was Jona, no longer in any coveralls or even white lab coat, but sitting in her jeans and grey t-shirt, glasses on, and typing furiously.

'Hey,' said Hope walking into the office, 'how's things in the world of forensics?'

'Too busy. There's too much paperwork when you're in charge. I know most of it but when you're not the one who has to do it normally it takes a bit of getting your head around it. I should be finished soon though. I take it you were looking for a drink or maybe a bit of meditation time.'

'I'm actually looking for that cross. Did you get much of a chance to establish where it's from?'

'We were examining it and found nothing on it that indicated who had touched it or how long it has been buried. And no, as for the where's-it-from, that's priority tomorrow.' Jona looked up at Hope's begging face. 'Unless of course you want it tonight.'

'Sorry, but I do. I've been stuck on the manhunt and not doing what I do best and actually investigating. Macleod's got his new star, Stewart on that. Looks at things differently.'

Jona laughed at the impersonation. 'You need to be easy on him; he's under stress big time.'

'And we are not? Not much point getting a promotion to

Sergeant if I can't still produce the goods and crack the case.'

'Well, you have me for an hour at the most. I'm up at six and I need to get a decent sleep because I haven't stopped today. Let's hope I can sleep tonight as well. Although Macleod's face when he thought you and I were an item was priceless.'

'Yes,' said Hope, 'one I'll hold forever. He's so very staid at times. Really struggles with the whole diversity thing. Maybe that's why he's surrounded himself with women, and Ross, of course. Still he's given me my shot so let's take it. Let's see what we can find about this cross.'

Jona stood and made her way out into the main hall before bringing back the gold item and laying it, still in an evidence bag, on the table. 'You type,' said Jona, 'my back's shot.'

Sitting down, Hope placed her hands on the keyboard and Jona pointed to an application on the screen. Within a minute the pair were beginning their search through a database of stolen items that encompassed the last forty years.

'There is one strange thing,' murmured Jona, looking over Hope's shoulders.

'What's that?'

'Why is it on its own? Where is everything else with it? It seems a strange thing for this item after all the maps we have found and the hunting down and murders. I mean it's a sweet looking piece of gold work, but I don't think it's going to be worth more than maybe twenty thousand.'

Hope turned and looked up at her colleague who even with Hope sitting down did not stretch much above her head. 'Since when was twenty thousand not a worthwhile sum to kill for?'

'Well, you would know more about that than me but it's not a standout piece. I mean, it's not well known in the collector's world today. I keep up with these things and that's not something people would instantly recognise. Of course, if it's not been on the scene for a while . . .'

'There's a wide range of ages involved in this,' said Hope. 'Alasdair MacPhail was in the older generation; Karen Gibbons' mother was much older. Jane Thorne was not young. And then there's Mr Drummer or whatever he's actually called. He's certainly of an age.'

'Well the database is showing nothing so let's go wider. Maybe it wasn't from the UK,' suggested Jona. 'Maybe they brought it back from abroad. That might be why we don't recognise it. Click on the European database link.'

Hope selected the desired app and then input basic details before allowing the system to complete its search. As she waited, Jona disappeared out into the larger hall before coming back with two cups of tea. Hope gratefully took one and then noticed Jona looking intently at her mobile.

'Something important?'

'No, not case related. I have to move out of my digs in two weeks and I still haven't found anywhere new. I was hoping to buy but I haven't found the right place so I'm trying to rent but it's not going well.'

'Great time to have to be looking as well with all this dumped on your shoulders,' said Hope. Then she had a thought. 'Why not move into mine until you find somewhere?'

'I thought you had a man, Allinson, isn't it? Be a bit crowded with the three of us.'

'Oh, he doesn't live with me. We thought about it, but I'm not convinced he's the one yet. That sounds so Macleod, doesn't it? No living together until you're married and all that. I mean what's it take to move out if it goes wrong.'

'Takes a lot.' With that Jona turned away and Hope wondered

if she'd hit a sore spot.

'The offer's there, Jona. I'd benefit from having someone fun about the place. I don't have many female friends, or any friends really.'

'I suppose moving all the way up to Inverness meant starting again.'

Hope nodded but she knew it was not true and the real issue was she was a loner. But Jona was easy to have about and would stop Allinson from treating her house like his next home-to-be.

The screen beeped and Hope looked at the returned search results. There were over forty investigations in over ten countries with a missing cross. She sighed. It did not look as if she would get wrapped up by midnight.

'Why don't you head on, Jona, and I'll do this? I reckon it'll take a good two to three hours at least. And if we have to call someone, it'll be tomorrow. You go and get some rest.'

'Got a better idea,' said Jona and grabbed her mobile again. Jona smiled at Hope who looked back bemused and then smiled wistfully as Jona broke into a conversation with someone on the mobile in Japanese. At least Hope believed it was Japanese, but she could not be sure due to her abysmal knowledge of languages.

The conversation was intense and then Jona took a picture of the cross in the evidence bag. There was more heated discussion and then Jona turned to Hope and warned her to smile. The mobile was brought up and there was more excited talk. But the voice for all the pace it was going at sounded older and male. And then abruptly, the call was closed.

'Okay,' said Hope, 'that was a little weird.'

'Sorry, it's Grandfather. He wanted to know who he had

been woken up for at this late hour. I told him my gorgeous red-headed friend and he insisted on seeing you.'

'Okay,' said Hope a little bemused. 'And was he helpful?'

'Very, otherwise I wouldn't have shown him you at all. He's very clever and a bit of a genius when it comes to antiques. He was a professor in London but he's in Glasgow now, or on the outskirts of it. He said he has to meet you, though. But you don't have to; he's just an old man. Still sharp when his mind's on it though. Although these days with the Parkinson's, he does get tired quickly.'

'As much as he sounds like fun, Jona, what did he say? Did it help?'

'Yes, sorry, Grandfather is always fun but difficult. He says it's from Spain and he reckoned it was not a mere twenty thousand, but it could be a lot more. He suggested there was a major robbery in Madrid back in the seventies when a lot of artefacts that were of that type were taken. He thinks it was seventy-three but he's not sure. He also drifted into talking about flowerbeds and decent restaurants in Glasgow. He's not the most cogent at times these days.'

'He sounded cogent, going off like a train chatting to you,' said Hope, sounding encouraging.

'Yes, but unfortunately if you knew the language, you'd see that one sentence barely follows the other. And that's not the Parkinson's.' Jona raised her hand to her hair, twisting it and looked out to the quiet hall beyond the office. Then she broke into a quick grin. 'He also said I should move in with you.'

'Yeah, did he think we would get on?'

'No,' laughed Jona, 'he said it would be a great excuse to come visit you. He talked about impressing you with his car. He hasn't had one for thirty years.' Her laugh turned into a bittersweet raising of the eyebrows.

'The offer's there,' said Hope and returned to the screen looking for Madrid and the 1970s. About halfway down the lists, she saw an entry that made her sit up straight and click on the screen. 'Jona, he might have been right.'

Hope felt a hand on her shoulder and Jona's head appeared beside her, fixated on the screen. Sure enough, there was a robbery of a national museum in 1972 which involved the theft of a collection of gold pieces. The pieces were hundreds of years old and Hope clicked the inventory button with shaking hands. She could feel the excitement flow through her and Jona's grip on her shoulders grew tighter.

As Hope scanned the items, all detailed in a box format, her eyes simply swam at the information. Trying hard, she couldn't make head nor tail of the catalogue system and began to flop back into her seat in frustration. But Jona fired a finger at the screen.

'There, click that. Let's see a photograph.' The screen opened up into a large photograph as the button was clicked and Jona screamed with delight.

'That's it! That's the one, Hope.'

'Are you sure?'

'Of course, I'm sure. Look at it. The curvature is the same. Check for any markings.'

'You do it,' said Hope, excited but lost as to how to identify the cross as a match.

Hope stood up as Jona leaned across and stared at the screen. She then picked up the cross before turning to Hope and embracing her in a massive, dancing hug. Hope's arms wrapped around Jona's neck and she allowed herself a jump for joy before the two of them stopped and looked at each other. Together, they burst out laughing.

'I guess it's late,' said Jona. 'That was a bit . . . emotional.'
And she laughed again holding the cross in the evidence bag
up before her.

Chapter 15

Macleod pulled on his shirt and slowly did up the buttons as he looked at himself in the mirror. It had been a difficult phone call and not one he had wished to have before starting a long day on a case that was struggling to go anywhere. But when he had seen the picture on his smart phone of his smiling partner Jane, he had leapt to answer it. And the brief few seconds of conversation with her had been good. It was not what was said, just the sound of her voice.

But she was with Hazel Mackintosh, in a hotel room in Glasgow and the senior forensic officer was not in a good way. It seemed her obvious mortality was now playing on her mind in a way he knew well. After his wife's suicide back on Lewis all those years ago, he tried to fathom where she had gone, where anyone went after they died. Some had told him because she died at her own hand she was lost, gone to whatever hell existed on the other side. Having been brought up in a Christian faith that offered the reward of heaven, he had been faced with the other side of the equation, the hell that pushed so many into a declaration of faith.

No, that was harsh. He had never been scared into believing in his God. But he had more questions than answers these days and maybe that was right. Mackintosh had never spoken of her beliefs on what came after this life, but she was definitely afraid of what it may hold. Or maybe she was just afraid of losing this world. But in her hour of anguish she was looking to him. A solitary woman who had briefly flirted his way, had now dropped the whole weight of her fears on his shoulders, when Jane, good and supportive as she was, seemed too aloof to the woman. Well, they barely knew each other. Hazel and he had at least some connection.

Stood in his shirt and underpants, Macleod looked at himself in the mirror. His legs were blotchy in places, just old skin that was now beyond renewing itself to those glorious days of his twenties. The hair was thinner and had less of a gleam to it. And then he thought of Hazel Mackintosh, who for all her years, and she was probably around his age, had such life about her. It would be such a waste. And he'd seen too many examples of the waste of a human life in his job. Sometimes he wished he had been a plumber or a person who fixed things. Seeing too much death could kill you.

Pulling on his trousers, Macleod sat down on the bed to put on his shoes. As he began to tie them, he thought of Hope who was seeming somewhat annoyed with him these days. The hunt for the suspects on Barra was not going well in the sense that it had not found any trace of them but that was not her fault. But every time she looked at him these days he thought he saw a scowl, anger at his decisions to keep her here with him. Was she right to be vexed? He hoped not. Stewart had a ferret nose and would come through whereas Hope was needed here, keeping everything tight.

It struck him how his mood could be so easily lifted or dropped by women, and not in any seedy way. Ross could appear in the office, and he was a decent man, all smiles and full of the joys of spring and it would not have affected Macleod's mood one iota. But if Hope appeared looking fresh-faced and beaming, or even that Jona Nakamura, his spirit would lift. Even when Mackintosh had been flirting with him, trying to steal something from him, he had been picked up despite making sure his refusal was understood. And as for Jane, she could change him in an instant. Were men fickle, or was the programming different and something to thank the manufacturer for?

With these thoughts in his head, Macleod walked down to the breakfast tables and saw Jona Nakamura. She was sitting with a colleague from the forensic team and it was her male companion who looked up and acknowledged Macleod first. Nodding politely back, Macleod sat down, then to be greeted by a smile from Jona and a query into how he was doing. Spirit lifted, he thought, and it was.

Twenty minutes later, Macleod stood over his desk looking at the pieces of map they had recovered during the course of the investigation. Hope was in the next room, organising the search for the young murderers of Karen Gibbons and he could hear the occasional agitation in her voice. His spirit descended a little and he knew he was fickle.

Across the room, he saw yesterday's paper and the folded sheets had the headline facing the ceiling. 'The Pirate Club.' It was apt due to the digging and Macleod was struggling to understand why items would be buried on beaches. Jona Nakamura had explained over breakfast the discovery Hope and she had made the previous night and so he knew that the items were not some long-buried treasure from a more primitive age. No, this was a modern crime, in the sense that it was within fifty years at least, so why bury the items and mark them with a map, albeit a map that was split up into many pieces? And not just in terms of the cartography but rather in that you would need all the pieces to locate the start point to your mission.

Dusty's Harbour, thought Macleod; *where was Dusty's Harbour?* If he could work out the start point, then he might have a chance of finding the items everyone was looking for before them and then maybe have a better lead to who was involved. *Well, who was involved, Seoras?*

Alasdair MacPhail, MOD singer and married to a crook, Maureen Ghillies, who was now dead and whose kids were looking for the treasure. He hated it calling it that, but it was the word on everyone's lips. Jane, the Canna victim who's address and name were wrong but who had a map. There was the old man, Dickerson or Drummer. That was three at least.

Then there was Karen Gibbons, murdered, and her mother who died from the shock of her daughter's death. Another part of the plot and maybe they were part of the group for she was out digging when she died. So at least four bits of map, maybe more. And who put the treasure where it now lies?

If you were going to hide something as an individual, why would you have a number of maps all spread out amongst different people? Surely one map with some sort of code only you knew how to decrypt would be more obvious—unless it was a team that was hiding loot. Given that the cross was such a recognisable item back then, maybe the treasure was hidden away for later onward sale.

'Sir,' announced Hope after rapping the door and entering.

Macleod held up his hand. 'A moment.' His eyes moved from the maps on his desk to the paper. *Pirate club. Maybe the paper was right—it was a pirate club, all waiting to get the loot after hiding it. And like all pirates, they want more than their fair share.*

'Sir.'

'Sorry, McGrath, what is it?'

'I'm heading out, sir; we might have a potential sighting and I'm going to check it.'

Macleod could see Hope's shoulders slump and her face was sullen. 'How many possible sightings is that now?'

'Four, all nothing. The papers have got this into people's heads. They are likely to start seeing Blackbeard at any moment.'

Raising his shoulders Macleod nodded his head in agreement. 'True but we need to check them all.'

Hope shut the door behind her. 'Permission to speak freely, sir.'

'You don't need to take that tone,' said Macleod. 'When it's the two of us, it's Seoras, Hope. You can say the difficult things to me; you are my Sergeant.'

'Exactly, so why is it you send our newest member of the team on the trail and have me looking after the bread and butter? Over on the mainland's where it's going to be solved. Why did you want me to take the damn exam? So you could have a lapdog? Someone to take care of you round here.'

'Stop!' Macleod stood up and in his throat were words of anger. She had no right. The decision of where to employ his team was his, and his alone. 'Sit down.' His words were calm, but firm. Yet inside, Macleod was raging. *Look beyond this,* he told himself.

When Hope had sat down, Macleod stepped out of the office and made two coffees before returning and placing a mug before Hope.

'I didn't want a coffee,' she spat.

'No, but I needed some time. You ever give me a load of abuse like that again and I will demote you back down to constable. You don't think I ever get riled at the Chief Inspector. Some days I could throttle her if I'm truthful but she's the position and the position deserves respect, even if you don't think much of the person.'

Macleod's calm was coming at a price. If he had been giving Hope the 'hairdryer treatment', as his old boss had called it, then the personal disappointment in her he felt would have been thrust to one side. But instead his spirit was definitely sinking.

'I apologise,' Hope forced out. It had no sense of sincerity, but Macleod was more concerned at his colleague's almost utter loss of professionalism.

'You are here because I need you here, Hope. God knows there's too much on my plate at the moment and I need an experienced set of eyes running over everything with me. I'd rather be over on the mainland too, but right now with how public this is becoming, I need you here. I have an inexperienced senior forensic officer and barely a team here on the island. They don't see many murders on Barra.'

'But you sent Stewart over there; she's hardly experienced. And that's where we will crack this case—you know that, don't you!'

'Keep the voice down. Of course, I know that, and she has the nose of a blood hound, Hope. She's right where I need her, as are you.'

Hope shook her head. 'The girl's inexperienced.'

'Which is why Ross is with her. Ross is solid, dependable, if not the most innovative. And he'll keep her safe. I rate Stewart, she's got a real mind for picking out detail but she's still raw, doesn't have the street smarts that you or Ross have.'

'Yes, but—'

'Don't but me! I know you're frustrated with this, but this is not you, Hope. You're more professional than this. What's really up? Is it Allinson?'

Hope flopped back into her chair. 'I don't know. I don't even want to ring him. I've had more fun with Jona over these last few days than I have with Allinson this last month. I came up here for him; he moved jobs for me. And then it's all gone sour. It's three-month McGrath again. I can't hold a relationship for more than ninety days.'

'Just be careful with Jona; she's young, and under pressure.'

Hope burst out laughing. 'We're not an item, Seoras. Just friends. Nothing sexual, just girlfriends.'

Macleod blushed. Twenty years ago, he wouldn't have had the idea in his head but with how diverse you have to be these days, he tried to be non-judgemental about these things. Now he was seeing them where they didn't exist.

'Keep plugging away on the search because this is where it will all play out. They will either get the loot from under our noses and leave more bodies, or we will find them and stop them. Let Ross and Stewart get on with their bit. I have a team, Hope, and I can't just have everyone where they think they should be. As for Allinson, whatever you do about it, do it soon because you're bringing it into work.'

Hope nodded and then made to get up before looking at Macleod. 'You said you had things on your plate? Want to share?'

Macleod stood and turned away for a moment running an

anxious hand through his hair. 'Believe me, Hope, if I could share I would but that's not my decision. I have to carry this one. One day you'll have it too, when you are in my shoes.'

'Okay.' And she was gone. Macleod never saw her face as she left to know just how she had really taken his talk. He knew Hope was feisty, but she was better than this. Allinson must really be affecting her.

Taking a large sip of coffee, Macleod looked down at the photocopies of the map pieces on his desk. Why Barra? What made Alasdair MacPhail look on Barra? And Karen Gibbons, as well? He could not see how to arrive at that conclusion. Why not Canna? They had found the cross on Barra, so surely the rest was there.

Macleod had kept the find of the cross quiet, lest they became inundated with the public and their metal detectors but there must have been other knowledge beyond the maps that led the victims in their search. But where was it? If only he had Karen Gibbons or her mother still alive. Or Mr Drummer, or whatever he was calling himself—he could question and prod for answers. But the trail was cold unless Stewart came up with something. He really had put a lot on her. The woman saw things Hope and he did not. But Ross was with her for guidance, and that should be enough. Because if it was not, then Hope needed to find him some suspects and quick.

Macleod felt the vibration in his pocket of his mobile phone and pulled it out. Jane's face was before him, with that tilt of the head and a cheeky look, the one where she would be teasing him before some *private time* as she was apt to refer to it. Hope had been blissfully unaware of that reason when Macleod had told her to put that image of Jane on the mobile. But he knew this call would not be about private time.

'Seoras?' It was Jane's voice.

'Yes, love.'

'Have you got five minutes? I know you're really busy and that, but I have Hazel with me and we're about to leave the hotel but she's not in a good way. I've tried talking with her and that but haven't got a real rapport with her. Not like you. Can you give her five minutes?'

Macleod looked at the maps before him and watched the busy room through the clouded glass door beyond his temporary office and saw so much work. He did not have time—he really did not. And it was a conversation he was not wanting. But sometimes things were beyond that of a police officer and work. The woman needed him, and his partner was urging him to speak to her.

'Just a minute.' Macleod placed his mobile on the desk and popped his head out of the front door telling the constable nearest to him that he was to be undisturbed for the next twenty minutes unless it was critical that he was seen. With that, he shut the door and walked back to the desk, picking up his mobile slowly. After telling Jane he was ready, he heard Hazel Mackintosh come to the phone and then through a mess of tears and snorts, he heard her unpack her fears and anxieties about the day ahead.

'It's going to be hard, Hazel, but you can tell me. I'm right here.'

Chapter 16

'Who's next on your list?' asked Ross.

'Simon Green, lives on the edge of Newcastle. Apparently, he was linked to a number of jobs MacPhail's wife took part in. He was a getaway man and has been quiet for a number of years.'

'Punch it in the Satnav for me and we'll get there sharp,' said Ross. 'Let's hope it's not a urine-filled flea hole like the last one we were in.'

Stewart smiled and then pushed back her glasses, before typing the postcode into the car's Satnav display beside her. At the moment she was feeling good, deep in the trawl of potential suspects, filtering through the debris, something she was good at. Ross was also a perfect companion. He said little but was calm and professional and also her equal. It felt like she did not have to impress him, unlike Macleod or McGrath. Although they had seemed happy with her work and had brought her on board, she had this desire to prove herself to them. But that was silly, and she knew it though it did not stop her from feeling it.

'Are we in a 1960s movie, Stewart?' asked Ross as the car pulled into the street the Satnav had directed them to. 'It's a bit grim. Feels like there should be a coal mine here.'

After a cold start between them, Ross was also becoming more familiar but not overly so. He exuded a calm demeanour in just about everything—unlike her bosses who could fire off at times. But then, they were carrying the can for these investigations. 'It's just up on the right, Ross.'

Ross parked the car at the end of a stone driveway that led to a semi-detached house. The house had seen better days and was made of red brick with white painted stonework under the windows. The paint was peeling and exposing the grey brickwork beneath, giving the place an air of abandonment. A green door with only a single number on it was slightly ajar. There should have been two numbers but only the screw holes remained of the first number.

Stewart heard her feet crunch on the stones as they approached, and she rapped the door causing it to open a touch further. To one side of the exposed hallway she saw a pile of envelopes, junk mail, and the like, simply lying on the carpet. A few coats were hung on basic pegs and the stairs to the upper floor could be seen, protected by a flaking white banister.

'Just a minute. Eating my tea.'

A minute later a man of maybe forty opened the door fully in a dressing gown that was falling open, exposing a pair of boxer shorts underneath and a hairy belly. His hair was blonde and long but beginning to thin. Announcing himself with a mighty belch, he then took a swig of his tin of beer. Stewart did not recognise the brand, but it looked like something you get cheap, tastes like rubbish, but is high enough in alcohol content that by the second or third you could not care less.

'Detectives Stewart and Ross, sir. We are looking for Simon Green.'

'Dad? What the hell do you want Dad for? He's long out of

that game. Paid his dues for a few years too. Leave him alone; he's clean now, not been near anything criminal for years.' The man started to raise his shoulders in an attempt to look slightly threatening but there's only so much threat you can conjure when your boxer shorts have a comic aardvark on them.

'We didn't say he was, sir. But we need him to help with our enquiries about something from the past. He may be in danger.' Stewart reinforced this statement with a serious look over the top of her glasses.

'Why?' asked the man, more concerned now.

'Do you know Alasdair MacPhail or his wife?'

'I don't. But dad might. He doesn't really talk to me about the old days. All he ever says is that he's glad he's out of it, but it set us up. Sometimes I think he's loopy; how is this place set up?'

Stewart glanced at Ross who gave the smallest of nods. 'Where is your father?' asked Stewart.

'At the social club, as they call it now. A working man's club really. I don't go. But in its day, Dad was always there with Mum, a place to be seen back then. But it's all he has of her now. Goes there for a pint and some dominoes with some of the old guys.'

'Do you have an address?' asked Stewart.

'No need. Down the road, take a right then an immediate left and you'll see it. *The Fallen Punter* is what it's called now, a bit of a joke from the new owners a few years back but it stuck.'

'Thank you,' Stewart said as she turned away to the car.

'Hang on. What's this all about. Why's everyone want Dad today?'

'Everyone?' said Ross turning on his heel. 'Who else has

been asking?'

'Girl came by about an hour ago, asking. Only a teen but man she was dressed to kill. Kept her talking just to stare at her rack. And she knew too, happy to let me chat away. Wriggled that arse on the way down the path, too.'

Ross did not say another word but ran. Stewart turned to the man in his doorway. 'What did she look like, hair, eyes, and that? What was she wearing too?'

Before he could answer, Ross howled at Stewart. 'Car, now!'

Ross never spoke harshly or in a raised tone, so the current instructions scared Stewart to her core. Without waiting for further from the man in the doorway, she bolted to the car and threw herself into the passenger seat. The car was racing away before she could apply her belt.

Ross threw the car around the corners as Stewart fired on the blue lights and the wailing siren. It was a drive of two minutes before Stewart saw the sign outside a rather drab building that said, *The Happy Punter*. A cheery face was splashed on the sign beside the words.

Ross was out of the car before Stewart and simply burst through the double doors at the front of the building. Stewart followed him along a bland corridor before Ross knocked a single door nearly off its hinges as they entered a bar area.

'Police! Peter Green, where is Peter Green?'

Before them was a room of older men, totalling six in number and all with a pint before them. The shock on their faces was palatable and Ross strode up to them and repeated his question. 'Peter Green, where is he?'

A man with white hair pointed towards a door at the rear of the building. 'He went with her. She was charging only a tenner. I'm next. You hear me, I'm next.'

142

Ross was already across the room before the man finished his sentence and Stewart followed him. As Ross broke through the door, he dove to the ground. Emerging into the outside air, Stewart saw Ross holding a man tightly with blood pouring from his throat. In the distance, she saw a teenage girl, possibly the one she had seen at Maureen Ghillies, disappearing into the fields behind the club.

'Go!' shouted Ross, 'Get her!'

Stewart did not hesitate and immediately ran after the girl, making her way straight out into the field. The long grass was wet, and she nearly slipped but hoped she would catch the girl who was wearing knee-length boots. The girl was making for a copse of trees and Stewart could see she had a mobile phone attached to her ear as she ran.

Stewart was fit and she was making up ground on the girl. The copse was still a distance away but if she kept up the pace, Stewart reckoned she would have the girl just as they reached the trees. Up ahead the girl tucked her mobile away and began running harder, a black skirt disappearing up above her backside. She really had been dressed like some sort of hooker, probably to entice the old guys. Although everyone talked about this girl as if she were always like that. Debbie MacPhail, in the flesh, thought Stewart, and I'll have her in cuffs within a few minutes.

The girl disappeared into the trees only ten metres ahead of Stewart. Racing in hard, Stewart was caught by an extended arm causing her to swing around it as it caught her throat, feet flailing out before her, and then crashing to the ground. Before she could react, stunned as she was, a male face appeared in her vision, followed by a fist which drilled into her face twice.

Stewart was used to taking a punch, but she had no protection and she struggled to stay conscious. As her head swam, she heard a female voice complaining she had been seen.

'No,' said a man, 'we don't kill police. They hunt you down. She won't know you from Adam, she only saw your back.'

'Easier to gut her now, or just a slice across her throat.'

'No. Let's go.'

Stewart's eye began to focus, and she saw the girl grab the man, planting a kiss on him and then pulling him tight, trying to get him to fondle her.

'Not pigging' now, Debs. We need to go.'

Stewart lay still, partly because she was so disorientated but also because she knew moving might cause a different reaction to running away, one that might end in her death. The couple disappeared out of the copse and Stewart tried to breathe easier. Her head was ringing, and she knew if she had been in the ring at her mixed martial arts club, the instructor would be in, pulling her opponent away from her. It was a hell of a punch.

It was maybe a minute later that she felt strong enough to stand up. Gathering her breath but still feeling a touch woozy, Stewart staggered through the copse and saw a drop on the other side down to a car. Beside the car, she saw the girl, dressed in black leather, skirt halfway up her backside and a top that simply presented her cleavage to all and sundry. Stewart was disgusted by her outfit, never mind her penchant for murder. And then she saw the blood across the girl's chest. Where was the man who had punched Stewart? Beside the girl, she saw a body.

For a moment, the girl looked up and saw Stewart. In her hand was a knife, covered in blood. The girl turned as if she were about to climb the slope. Stewart gathered all the strength she had and stood tall, fists before her in a fighting stance she had learned over the last three years at her club.

'Come on,' cried Stewart, a wild look in her eye and she briefly pushed her glasses back onto her face. It was then she realised that one of the lenses was cracked but she never flinched. Beneath her, the girl licked her lips. Assessing her, knife in hand.

'Next time, bitch.' The girl jumped into the car and drove off as Stewart collapsed to the ground and sat on her bottom hands in her head. She thought about the punch that had laid her out, about the conversation between the man and Debbie MacPhail. How he had stopped Debbie killing her. And then she began to sob. It had been so close. She would have been dead. And her brother, with all his difficulties would be alone, with only what little help they got from the council. Her body shook as the tears flooded from her.

Ross watched Stewart take off after the girl before turning back to the man in his arms. He was starting to gurgle, his throat pouring blood. In an instinctive response, Ross placed his hands over the aperture in the neck. The gurgling continued but it was less harsh. The man's eyes rolled and his body jerked. Ross knew he had to keep him awake.

A number of the patrons from the working men's club emerged from the back door and were visibly shocked. Hands over mouths and the occasional cry were of no use to Ross and he shouted at the small crowd to ring for an ambulance.

'Come on, Simon; stay with me,' urged Ross. The man's eyes suddenly focused and he lifted a hand only for it to drop back down again. 'That's it, ambulance is on its way. Stay with me and we'll sort you, you hear me! Stay with me, Simon.'

'Who was she?' croaked the man.

'MacPhail's daughter, Simon,' said Ross and looked to the man's stomach where blood was beginning to soak through his clothing. *Where the hell's the ambulance?* Ross knew this was an unreasonable statement but the fear of losing this man had just jumped tenfold on seeing the blood now coming from his torso. Ross' own hands ran red with the crimson liquid from the man's neck and his own heart was beating ten to the dozen.

'MacPhail?' croaked Simon Green. 'But she was so willing.' The words were rasped, fighting to the surface of forced breaths. 'My map, she came for my map.'

Ross was torn between trying to keep the man in a calm state and give him the best chance to survive and getting information from him before he potentially died. Looking at the figure, he made the horrible decision that he was looking at the last minutes of the life of Simon Green and tried to sort his thoughts for the very few questions he would get a chance to ask.

'Did she get the map?'

'No,' came a croak, 'I tore it up. Have it in my head, you see.' The man's head rolled to one side and Ross repositioned himself to shift it back into a position where he could maintain his grip on the neck. But the air was still coming out through the side. He would need to be intubated or whatever they called it. Ross saw the eyes swim again and pressed on with his questions.

'What is hidden?'

'Proceeds from our great robbery. Spain, we did it.' There was an attempted laugh that ended in coughing.

'Who did it?'

'MacPhail, Gibbons, Tao, Dudley, old Dudders, and me.' Ross

thought he saw a smile on the man's lips even as he struggled for breath, like a sense of pride coming to him. 'MacPhail's kid, like her mother. Cold hearted bitch but sexy as . . .'

Simon Green slumped again, and Ross slapped his face with one hand while still holding his neck. There was a small crowd around him and he heard someone say the ambulance was coming.

'What did you do with the loot from the Spanish job?' asked Ross. 'Did you all have a map?'

'Five . . . five maps.'

'But who buried it?' Ross was confused as to how none of them knew where it was. Someone had to have buried the loot.

'MacPhail . . . got an explorer.' Green's breathing was now becoming a torrid affair, his words coming out in brief gasps. Ross saw the end coming for the man.

'What's his name?'

'Her . . . Wall . . . Young woman . . . Wall.'

'But MacPhail's kids, they don't have your piece of the map? They can't find the loot?'

'Yes . . . Dusty's . . . Harbour. It's on . . . my map.'

'Where is it? Where's the harbour?'

'She . . . stayed . . . with me. Beautiful . . . but MacPhail . . . made . . . her stay . . . stay with me.'

The eyes rolled again and Ross tried to slap the man back to the moment but there was no response; his breath became even weaker and as Ross watched, the body seemed to shut down, giving out only the occasional jerk of involuntary motion. As the paramedics arrived, Ross believed there was no life left.

'Is it always this rough in the Highlands?' said a Geordie voice and Stewart looked up into the eyes of an older man. He sported a white beard and looked like an out-of-work Santa Claus. 'DI Callen. Are you okay, Detective?'

Stewart nodded and stood up. She had been waiting for the local force to arrive after calling them and had stayed with the body of the man Debbie MacPhail had dispatched with such cold brutality. One moment stimulating his sexual hunger then turning him and slitting his throat. The woman's eyes were still on Stewart's mind and she shivered when she remembered the standoff. *It had been too close, too damned close.*

'We'll take care of the scene, Detective, but I'll need you to make a statement, of course. Shall we join your colleague back at the club? You look like you could do with some support from a friendly face.'

Half in a daze, Stewart sat in the rear of the police car looking out the window but seeing nothing. When they arrived at the club, she saw Ross making a statement, his shirt and suit covered in blood. Someone handed her a cup of tea and she sat along from Ross and told her story to the DI. When she was complete, she found Ross waiting for her.

'You okay?' he asked.

'No. Are you?'

Ross smiled. 'Not really. He died right in my—'

'She was going to kill me,' blurted Stewart. 'He stopped her, and she just slit his throat. I had to stand, or she was coming for me. Going to slit my throat.' Stewart pitched forward grabbing hold of Ross who embraced her. Floods of tears came out and she held him tight as all the fear exploded from her body.

'She didn't, and you're here. It's okay.' Taking her face in his hands, he tilted it back and she looked up into a concerned face. 'Did she hit you like that?' Stewart wondered what her face looked like. Her cracked lens in her glasses must have given her the look of the weedy nerd at school but she felt the smarting cheekbone from the punch. It must be coming up in a cracking bruise. She buried her head back in his chest and ignored the dried blood on his shirt.

After a few minutes, Ross made her sit down on a nearby step and joined her. 'He gave me all the names of the group that did the robbery. I noted them down. 'MacPhail, Gibbons, Tao, and Dudley. We need to get onto those, see if they have connection to the Spanish robbery Nakamura spoke of.'

'There was little when they checked about the robbery, so it's unlikely to yield much,' said Stewart, feeling extremely flat.

'No, but think about it. They are all running around looking for map pieces. Someone had to bury the loot from the robbery in the first place. So, someone had all pieces of the map, probably drew up the map so they all had to go back together. Green said it was a woman who hid it all. Name of Wall.'

'We need to search his house for anything; he must have a map.'

'He has no map because he destroyed it. But his map had Dusty's Harbour on it and he knew the location. Debbie MacPhail forced it from him. If they get the other maps, then they will have all the pieces. They have MacPhail's—Gibbons' too after that night on the beach. Tao must be our Canna victim and I reckon Dudley is the old guy on the loose on Barra. They can't be far off succeeding.'

Stewart nodded, the information bringing her back into focus about the job. Chewing over the detail, she stood up and then helped Ross to his feet. 'Then we need to get to Simon Green's house and search it. It's all we have over here. Maybe he kept a copy hidden away. He wouldn't destroy the map—surely he's bluffing.'

'Let's get to his house and find out,' smiled Ross. 'And Kirsten, I'm sorry; I shouldn't have left you out there alone.'

'You were cradling a dying man; It's hardly your fault.' But his face said different.

Chapter 17

Hope cursed the day as she stood in Castlebay looking out at another dreich day. If these murderers, or even the one they called Dudley, were on Barra, they were keeping a heck of a low profile. They had searched the whole island, going house to house; the uniforms had done what they could and various teams from the other agencies had helped cover the open ground, but still nothing. She could see Macleod was getting tetchy, anxious that they were not going forward. On the brighter side, there was such a presence that there was no way the people she sought could come out in the daylight without being noticed, or so she hoped.

Despite sticking to the job and keeping her professionalism after Macleod's rebuke, Hope was angry. She hated this organising, this pulling of the resources around. Instead she wanted to be out there, like Stewart. *Sounds like she had quite a time down in Newcastle from what Ross said. Should have been me.*

'Hey!' It was Jona Nakamura exiting from the small police station, dressed in a t-shirt and jeans. The diminutive woman still looked smart despite her more casual clothing. Since taking over from Mackintosh, Jona had been dressing in a snappy fashion, showing she was the boss and lead. But this time she had been called from her examinations and hence was less smartly dressed. Hope thought she suited the more casual look.

'You okay?' asked the Asian woman. 'I just spoke with Macleod and when I talked about passing the information I had for him to you, he seemed a bit distant. You two okay?'

'Just a lover's tiff,' Hope replied and then grinned. But she could not hold the smile for long.

'What's the real issue? If you want to tell me, of course.'

'Just everything. Him,' Hope pointed at the station. 'Allinson, these bloody murderers, and Stewart getting all the fun. Sound like a jealous, cranky bitch, don't I.'

Jona stood in front of Hope and took one of her hands before staring up into her face. 'Damn right you do. And I think you're a bit better than that.' She took Hope's other hand. 'Look, you can't do anything about Macleod's decision, and I think he's under other pressures. I'm not sure what's up with Hazel but she was not good when she last spoke to me and she was confiding a lot in the DI, so just forget how he is and cut him some slack.'

'Maybe, but—'

'No buts, girl. As for Allinson, you can't sort that until you get back. Stewart's work is not your decision either, so focus on what you can change. Find MacPhail's kids. Find the old man.'

Hope turned away. 'There's not a lot of point. They've gone to ground. We 've looked everywhere, Jona.'

'Then look differently at it.' Jona grabbed one of Hope's hands again. 'Meet them where they are going to be. Solve these damn maps. Come on, this isn't the woman that raced after those kids when we were out on the beach in the dark watching Gibbons. You're better than this.'

Hope turned her head and saw a stern pair of eyes. Allinson was fun, complimentary and steady but Jona seemed unafraid to go into Hope's darker places. Something welled up inside Hope and she struggled to contain a wide beaming smile which was begging to race out from her. Right now, she wanted to embrace Jona, hold her tight and tell her just what a friend she was being. And that it felt like more than friendship to Hope. But that was not what Jona was offering, so Hope gave only a forced grin and a resolute face.

Jona reached up and gave Hope a simple hug and Hope hugged back gently, resisting the urge to hold Jona far tighter. When they released, they both stood looking a little ridiculous.

'Got to get back to work,' said Jona.

Hope nodded and watched her go. Before she could have any deeper thoughts about Jona, she forced herself to look away to Kisimul Castle, lonely in the bay, the damp day unable to stop the ancient structure looking impressive. And that's all it was, just a dreich day in her career, one of many to come no doubt. But there was no option other than to stick on a jacket and get on with it.

They had combed the island and found nothing. Jona said they should meet the killers, get to where they would be by solving the maps. Well, Macleod was sitting with the maps and getting nowhere without a key. Dusty's Harbour was the place that might solve it? But maybe there was more she was overlooking. Recover the ground—go back and look again.

Popping inside the station, Hope gave out instructions about where to find her if the search teams found anything and then half walked and half ran to the community hall the forensic team were set up in. As she walked in, she saw Jona Nakamura

153

busy ushering her people around. The woman looked up and smiled when she saw Hope, walking across directly to her.

'How can I help you, Sergeant?' asked Jona, keeping a professional air while beaming at Hope's arrival.

'I need to look at the items found with the bodies—everything that was on them.'

'Looking for anything in particular?'

'No,' said Hope, 'just going over the ground again. Looking for something we haven't seen.'

'I'll accompany you.'

Inside Hope glowed as Jona said she would assist but her mind said that would be a distraction and as much as she enjoyed Jona's company, along with all the feelings she could not fully rationalise about her at this time, she knew, professionally speaking, Jona had better things to do and Hope would work quicker without her.

'Just give me one of your bods, Jona,' said Hope quietly. 'You have plenty to do; I don't want to keep you back.' Jona looked torn but agreed and called over a man in his thirties with dark hair and a left eye that seemed to be only half opened. Peters was introduced to Hope and then led her to a small room at the rear of the hall.

Before Hope was a small array of items including clothing and personal effects of the deceased found on Barra, along with a package of photographs of the items and clothing found on the Canna victim. In truth there was not a lot, with the majority of the effects belonging to the Gibbons. After donning the necessary gloves and protective clothing, Hope searched through dresses and suitcases trying to find anything that had been overlooked. Item by item she took them in hand and then discarded them back to their places when they seemed to be shedding no further information.

A dress that spoke of a conservative woman, the colours simple and plain. A packet of condoms in Karen Gibbons' suitcase that confirmed she was happily looking for someone to copulate with. There was always the question as to whether Karen had simply met Alasdair MacPhail, but the condoms gave the impression that her energetic meeting was with a sought-out partner rather than a wholly random occurrence. Or maybe she was just a careful planner. Placing the small plastic bag on the table, Hope picked up another containing a delicate bracelet with a number of charms on it. Karen had not been wearing the bracelet, it was just one of the items collected from her room.

'Peters, has this been run against the items stolen in the Spanish job?'

'Yes, there were no charm bracelets found on the list.'

'Hope held the bracelet up, letting the items dangle from it. She saw an elephant, a silver kite-shaped object with a diamond in the end of it, a green emerald in a tiny carriage. As the items swung off simple silver connectors to the bracelet, Hope realised that they all dangled at slightly different lengths. Not one corresponded in length to the other as they swung. Yes, they all had silver elements to them, but Hope struggled to see the connection.

'Is that normal, Peters?' asked Hope. 'Can you see how they all don't line up. If I dangle them, they are all at different heights. Not one the same. Is that unusual?'

'I really couldn't say. But they are all on the same bracelet. Maybe they're not meant to be.'

'Bit strange to me. Can you tell me anything about the bracelet, if it matches the items hanging from it? I mean in composition. We could take it for an analysis but that would be a bit unusual to take parts of it and break them down for analysis. It is only a bracelet.

Damn it, there's got to be something here, thought Hope, *but I can't see anything else.* 'Can you get me Jona?' Hope watched a startled expression come across Peters' face. 'Sorry, Miss Nakamura, can you get her for me?'

Hope held the bracelet to the light as Jona entered the room. She saw Jona's perplexed face and smiled at the woman in the open white lab coat.

'Peters says you want to break some of my items apart for analysis.'

Hope grinned. 'Am I causing trouble?'

'I think you are trouble but what can I do for you?'

'Do you think this bracelet looks odd? None of the charms match in length if you hold the bracelet up. Is that not unusual?'

Jona stepped closer and bent until she was in line with the bottom of the dangling objects. 'Maybe, but all the connections are the same. 'Except . . .'

Hope watched Jona take the bracelet from her and begin to look at each charm individually. 'Except what?' asked Hope, starting to feel a glimmer of excitement.

'Too easy to miss because it's been done so well. If you look at the connections from the charms to the bracelet, the limbs connecting are all very standard and actually very plain. But where they hook onto the charms, that's a great piece of work. Someone has crafted an opening, an eye for the limb to hook onto the charm. The bridge where the limb hooks into is actually an addition and not the original casting. You could miss that so easily.'

Hope found herself bending closer to Jona and staring into

her face. 'So, what does that mean?'

'I'm not sure.' Jona turned to the open door and shouted, 'Peters, can you bring my laptop in here?'

While her device was brought in, Jona placed the bracelet on the table and slowly separated out each of the charms on it. 'Do you think you would recognise something great from something cheap, Sergeant? I thought I would have but this is so clever. Because none of it was uniform, it looks like a cheap bracelet. If something's not uniform then you assume it's added a charm from here or there, like you would have with a cheap bracelet. But this is no cheap bracelet. Well, actually the bracelet is but the charms I believe are the real jewels here.'

Hope leant over Jona's shoulder as she started to work on her laptop. The woman was going through the itinerary of the items stolen in the Spanish job from years ago.

'Look,' said Jona pointing at the screen, 'if you search for a charm bracelet there's nothing there and someone has assumed that the other pieces are all part of this. But they're not. Look at the elephant on the bracelet. And then look at the one on the screen.'

'That's a match,' shouted Hope a little too loudly.

Jona pulled her shoulders in and calmly pronounced, 'Yes, that is a match, Detective. And there's your emerald in the carriage. And there's the kite shape with the diamond. But that hippo is not there. Nor the clover leaf. I reckon they must be cover for the others.'

'There was the cross in the sand. You don't think they buried it in sporadic areas, a small part at a time?'

'Maybe. But you have many maps which don't show something obvious, or do they? Or do they know a reference point we don't?

'Dusty's bloody Harbour,' murmured Hope.

'I need to get back into this and sort out what item is what. You should take this to Macleod—might cheer him up.'

Hope looked to the side and noted Peters had left the room. In a moment of euphoria, she threw her arms around Jona and kissed her on the side of the head before quickly releasing. 'You did it, Jona,' she whispered. 'Thank you.'

Jona turned her head and gave Hope a look she had not seen before. There seemed to be no emotion in the face, neither happy nor sad, no shock or delight. Maybe she had gone too far.

'Macleod, Hope,' whispered Jona, 'take it to Macleod. And you did it. Happy to help but don't do that here.'

Hope reddened and nodded before striding off to Macleod. *She said not here, said nothing about elsewhere.*

Chapter 18

The night had fallen when Hope made her way back to the police station to look for Macleod. Inside she was bubbling, half excited by the case and half by her developing friendship with Jona. There was a confidence back in her stride and she breezed in through the door of the compact station and immediately sought Macleod out in his back office only to find the door locked.

'Does anyone know where the Inspector is?' she asked the room in a controlled but loud voice.

'Back at the hotel, Sergeant. I believe he's eating. At least that's what he said.'

Thanking the officer for this information, Hope turned on her heel and strode the short distance to the hotel, ignoring the drizzle that was beginning to fall. Although there were some streetlights, it was hard to see much along the road until a car passed by. Castlebay was similar in many ways to many of the towns and villages she encountered in the islands but the road through it was undulating and when the sun was up, you looked out onto a glorious bay and the iconic castle in the middle of it. But the night gave the place more of an edge. Maybe before when there were no murders committed in the area it would have seemed a quaint if wintry setting but now the shadows held possible menace.

The hotel was busy, an influx of visitors due to the sudden notoriety of the island in the current case and Hope did not see her boss at the first time of looking around the dining room. Taking a second look, she saw him in a far corner with a mobile phone attached to his ear. His face looked sullen. Before him was a half-eaten plate of beef which looked positively delicious to Hope. It had been a while since she had eaten, and the hunger pangs were beginning in her stomach.

'Sir—'

Macleod held up a hand to Hope and turned in his chair so his mouth was out of view. He was speaking in a whisper and Hope struggled to hear what he was saying. It was not that she wanted to eavesdrop but when your number one arrives with purpose what could be detaining him on the phone.

'I'm so sorry. Call me anytime.' Macleod turned back to Hope looking almost shell shocked. His face was white as if he had been passed by a ghost. At first, he did not look at Hope but instead took his coffee in his hand and drank from the cup in quick gulps. Hope swore his hand almost trembled.

'Are you okay, sir?'

'What? Yes, I'm okay, McGrath; just an old friend has had some bad news. Just poor timing, really, I guess.' He seemed slow, as if his mind were not fully in the moment. 'You just go along and then, wham, it blindsides you, Hope. Makes your view of people change when you see them for what they really are.'

Hope did not understand what her boss was talking about and tried to wait for an explanation, to allow him to engage her in his moment of difficulty but her earlier find was too much to hold back.

'Sir, Karen Gibbons, she had a charm bracelet which we decided was nothing when we looked at her effects recently but having had a closer look some of the charms are from that Spanish robbery. It's making me wonder just how this loot is all spread out. Is it in one place or do these maps give a number of locations because that is how they have spread out the stolen items? Maybe there isn't one single stash.'

'Slow down. And not here. Let's go through to the bar and get a quiet corner.'

Hope hopped from one foot to the other trying to contain her excitement. He had put her on search organisation and yet she was still coming up with the goods with regard to investigation of the recovered items. He'd know who his Sergeant was now. And then Hope watched Macleod simply leave half of his dinner on the plate and step away to the bar.

'Do you want anything from the bar?'

'Coffee, if you're having one, sir.'

'Okay, always good to have coffee with people.'

Hope stared at Macleod as he shuffled away. His shoulders were down, and he seemed morbid. Looking at the plate he had left behind, she saw the long slice of roast beef and looked around her quickly. *Oh, sod it.* With a fast hand she grabbed the slice and stuffed it in her mouth chewing in a rush to make the evidence vanish. After a quick wipe of her mouth and hands with a napkin, Hope strode into the bar after Macleod.

Macleod was sitting at a table in the far corner and there was only one table close to him where a dark-haired, older man was enjoying a pint of Guinness with a whiskey chaser beside it. He had dark, thick-rimmed glasses on that reminded Hope of Stewart, the new star of the team and she felt a little shock at how she felt a touch of spite. Was it Allinson that had made her lose her confidence, or was it disappearing already after leaving her Glasgow home? Heck, she was starting to imagine feelings to a woman who could not feel the same inclination towards her. But Jona was good for her, and she just wished she could be good for Jona too.

Hope slid in beside Macleod as two coffees arrived. He turned and tried to give Hope a smile, but it was as if the energy was not available for him to complete the task. Reaching inside his pocket, he took out some folded sheets of A4 and held them up so only Hope and himself could see them. On the sheet were various snapshots of the maps they had gathered so far.

'Tell me what you've discovered then,' said Macleod, sounding flat.

'I was going through the belongings of our victims again and came across a charm bracelet owned by Karen Gibbons. On closer inspection, it did not seem to have been put together right so I had Jona—sorry, Miss Nakamura look at it. She said that about half the charms are actually from the Spanish heist the cross is from. Because they looked like they were correctly attached to the charm bracelet, no one clocked them as individual items.'

'All right,' said Macleod, sipping his coffee and focusing in more, 'what does that help us with?'

'Just a hunch, but maybe the whole of the loot is spread about, here, there, and everywhere. Maybe that's why there's different positions on the map.

Macleod sat back and Hope could see he was in deep thought. For all that he was an older man stuck fighting to break free from earlier times and conventions, one thing he did have was a knack for spotting what was really going on. She had learnt to give him space to think because he was able to grasp the

162

reality of the situation with a fuller understanding than she did. After a few minutes, he shook his head.

'No. Not spread out, there's too much of it. Why just give everyone a map of a portion of the loot? They would have dug it up by now if they had hit hard times. No, something has them running for the treasure now. Something has made them wait.'

'Like what?'

'I don't know. Maybe they couldn't get a piece of the jigsaw. I mean it's been a long time since that robbery. They could have shifted the goods on by now. But there are these maps, handed out, a piece each. That's to keep them honest and in check, so they don't move it on before they have agreed to. But maybe there are pieces left out, put to one side for a rainy day, hidden but available to each of them.'

'So, what do we do with this?'

'What can we do, Hope? We wait for Stewart. She's at the source of this. Ross and her are close, so close they nearly got killed. There's nothing we can do. We either find the children of MacPhail running around here and that Dudley bloke, or we get to the loot before them. Listen to me. I've fought hard at every press conference to say *stolen items* and not loot and I'm beginning to talk like a pirate myself.'

'But why don't we take a look at our maps and see if we can find these smaller deposits? We could get ahead of them, we could . . .'

Macleod was not listening. Instead, he was focused on the man at the table next to them. Hope stopped herself from turning around fully to look. Instead, she brought her finger up to her chest and then pointed at the man but tight into herself so the man could not see what she was doing. Macleod gave an almost imperceptible nod.

Hope stood up quickly and spun around reaching out for the man. But his chair was already falling backwards, and he was halfway across the bar.

'Get him, McGrath, that's Dudley!'

Hope exploded into a run across the bar but caught the leg of a seat as an unsuspecting drinker moved back their chair. Tumbling forward, she clattered into a man carrying a tray of drinks which flew to the air. Beer landed on her neck and glasses smashed on the floor, but she picked herself up and continued to chase.

The man was out of the door and when she reached the outside of the street, she barely saw him in the poor light. But there was a foot and the sound of heavy breathing in the dark and Hope raced towards that sound. Along from the hotel was a loop of road that led down to the harbourside and her fleeing suspect had taken this route. Running hard, she sought him in the dark and could hear the gentle crash of the sea against the harbour walls.

A small outboard motor started and Hope left the road and moved onto the rocky shore, fighting to keep her footing on the wet rocks. There were a number of tenders nearby presumably from the yachts and motorboats who had arrived after the news of the first murders had leaked. Some would be treasure seekers, some just wanting in on the buzz of the situation but with the island packed, many had brought or hired yachts and boats and now filled the moorings just off the shore.

A grey dinghy was leaving shore and heading for Kisimul castle and Hope jumped into a similar tender and started the engine. She heard Macleod shouting for her to wait for him, but she was in pursuit. *I'll show him, bring back his suspect for him. Stewart's not the only one who can get into the field.*

It took only a few minutes for the suspect's tender to reach the castle, sitting out in the bay, dark as the night that now surrounded it. Hope struggled to see much as she landed her craft and then noticed a figure in the dark scrambling across the rocks. Jumping from her tender, Hope slipped on a seaweed covered rock and came down hard with a thump, her cheek crashing into a stone. The whole side of her body smarted but she got back to her feet and then as quickly as she dared, she began to cross the treacherous rocks until she got to the castle walls.

'Dudley, you bastard. We have you now. Pretty poor place to stash a map, especially for an old fart like yourself.'

The voice was young and male, and Hope slid along the castle walls until she could make out two figures in the dark. Th older man was standing upright with his hands raised, startled from the little Hope could see of his face. It was poorly lit by a torch held by the other man who was also holding a gun, the torch barely lighting the barrel but even Hope could recognise the shape.

'Map! Where have you stashed it? I know it's here some-where. Say or I'll kill you.'

'Kill me, then you won't have a map and no goods, son. I'm not stupid.'

'Then I'll shoot your kneecaps until you tell me. One by one so you can't walk. All the money in the world won't be any good when you have to crawl for your dinner.' With that the young man stepped forward and pointed the gun directly at Dudley's knees.

'Okay, I'll get it.'

Hope felt her heart beating hard, and the adrenalin begin to flow but she tried to hold herself in check, awaiting the correct moment to intervene. If she could get the map as well as both of these suspects, she'd show Macleod her worth.

Dudley walked a little further around the castle until he reached down into a gap in the rocks. At least that's how it looked to Hope as everything was so dark. Dudley threw a bag at the other man.

'There. Now piss off before they get here. I'm being pursued.'

The younger man seemed to panic. 'Pursued? Well then, end of the line, old man. Can't have any witnesses.'

Hope was already running from her position and threw herself at the younger man as a shot rang out in the night. But she must have caught him in time for she heard Dudley begin to run as she fell in a pile with the other man. Hope desperately got to her feet, scrambling for the gun that had fallen but could not find it among the rocks. Then she felt an arm around her throat and Hope clutched at it as she felt the breath leave her, not to be replaced. The grip was strong and she started to elbow him into his stomach with all she had. It took four blows before he backed off. As he did, they both saw Dudley grab the bag he had pulled from the rocks and start to run back toward the tender he had brought ashore.

The younger man moved to intercept but Hope blocked his path. 'Stand down. You're under arrest.' But the man did not wait and tried to run past Hope. She reached out for him and grabbed him by the arm spinning him round and forcing his arm up his back. But then her foot slipped on a patch of seaweed and she tumbled forward driving the man forward too but losing her grasp on him. The man reacted quicker and drove a foot at Hope's head, catching her left temple and stunning her in her prone position.

As she lay in the dark, the man ran off and she could hear another motor as he disappeared on another tender. Hope tried to stand but with the combination of her wooziness from the blow to the head and the seaweed covered rocks, she could only slip and slide until she fell down upon her bottom and chose to remain there. They were gone anyway; she'd never catch them now.

It was over ten minutes later when she heard a new engine and looked up to see torches. Giving a hoarse shout, Hope waved attention to her and looked up to see Macleod standing in a long coat and tutting to himself.

Kneeling down beside her, Macleod whispered in her ear, 'What are you doing? These guys are murderers; you need to take backup with you. I nearly lost Stewart earlier today. I don't need to lose you. Stop trying to impress; you are right where I need you, nothing more, nothing less. Now, report.'

Hope filled in Macleod, advising of the map that Dudley had and how the young man who she suspected was Andy MacPhail, had tried to kill Dudley. Around her, Macleod set the accompanying officers on a search for the gun. Leaving one of the uniformed sergeants in charge, Hope and Macleod returned to the hotel where they questioned the barman about the client who had run.

'Been here a few days but he doesn't tend to be in the bar like that, often keeping himself to himself and then disappearing out.'

Hope wondered if the man had been watching Macleod as he ate, or was it just chance he was in earshot of them when he ran? Either way, he was gone and their chance to grab one of the hunters of the treasure had vanished. Hope asked to see the man's bedroom almost as an afterthought as she doubted there would be anything of use left behind. Surely, he would be too careful about that, and besides, he had the map.

As they were shown to the room, Jona Nakamura appeared on scene dressed in a pair of jeans and a leather jacket. 'If you are going to take a look in that room, then can I kindly ask that I do the searching.' She threw them a pair of gloves each and then noticed that Hope had a badly bruised temple. 'You okay?'

Hope nodded and pointed to the now open door, allowing Jona to enter first. Macleod hung back and let the two women start to open drawers and wardrobes. There was a small amount of clothes in the room but that was almost the full extent of its contents. Macleod indicated that they should look in the en suite and Jona flicked the light switch. The room was clean and hardly used but there was an assortment of hygienic products for teeth and hair on the edge of the wash hand basin. Jona picked up each item turning it over before replacing it in exactly the same position. Until her photographer was here, she did want anything moved.

Macleod returned to the room and turned his attention to a small suitcase in the corner of the room. Jona had opened it and examined the objects saying there was nothing of note, only a shaver and some nail clippers. When Hope left the bathroom, she saw him standing there focused intently on the contents of the case.

'What, sir? What's the matter?'

'There's a shaver in the case,' said Macleod.

'And?' asked Hope in frustration at not seeing his thinking.

'There's a razor and shaving foam in the bathroom,' said Jona.

Turning back to the bathroom, Hope saw Jona bring out

the items in her gloved hand and delicately set them on the dressing table in the room. She held them up before her, turning them over and over again. The razor was held up, shaken and then placed back down. Then the shaving can was shaken. This time she shook it twice, and then a third time. Delicately she squirted a little of the foam out.

'That's squirting well for the amount in it. I think you may be onto something, Inspector.' Jona grinned and then pulled out a small knife from her jacket. Delicately, she examined the bottom of the can and then slid the knife along the edge before levering it against the bottom of the can. The bottom fell off suddenly, dropping with a clatter onto the table. A rolled-up piece of paper fell out too.

Hope reached forward but had her hand tapped aside by Jona's hand which held the knife. 'Gently, don't crease it.'

Hope picked up the paper and unravelled it, setting the small paper on the desk. The image had obviously been shrunk but it showed a map of the Isle of Barra and its associated smaller islands with a number of crosses on the map.

'It's going to be a late one,' said Macleod. 'Miss Nakamura, kindly get your photographer and get me pictures of that map that I can use before you do any other searching in this room. And Hope,' he said turning to his Sergeant, 'go get a shower and a change. I'm going to need you at the station in half an hour.'

With that Macleod walked out of the room, leaving the two women looking at each other. 'He's a bit sharp tonight,' said Jona.

'Not half, he gave me a bollocking at Kisimul Castle.'

'Got something on his mind, then. Outside of this as if it isn't enough. Let me get my team sorted and then I'll come sort you out with that bump on the head. It'll only take five minutes.' Hope saw Jona looking at her with concerned eyes. 'Are you all right, Hope?'

'No, Jona, I'm not. And I don't mean the bump on the head.'

Chapter 19

S tewart's face was smarting, but she had managed a quick change and a shower at the police station before Ross and she returned to Simon Green's home. His son was no longer there, having been taken away by the force to formally identify his father and there was a small crowd of locals hanging around. Several uniformed officers kept a guard line and let the highland pair through on production of their badges.

Her replacement glasses, which Stewart always carried with her, felt slightly uncomfortable on her nose. The style was exactly the same, but she believed that her first pair had worn some sort of groove around the bridge of her nose, as she slid them towards her eyes. The replacement would have to do but when she returned to Inverness, a priority would be made of getting a replacement lens for the original pair.

Ross strode up the driveway and noticed a lack of forensics but then again nothing had actually taken place at this run down semi-detached. Stepping into the hallway, Ross walked through to the kitchen at the rear of the house. Following him, Stewart saw the line of grease behind the electric hobs and a clogged-up extractor fan above them. There was an actual chip pan, complete with a depth of oil. Surely those death traps had been got rid of years ago, in a blast of healthy eating and a safety campaign to stop kitchen fires. Not here it seemed.

From the kitchen, they walked around the ground floor and took in a small dining room and front lounge, complete with a television that could display actors in an almost life-size proportion. Several cans of some cheap lager were lying around the couch. It was not the classiest house Stewart had ever examined.

After taking the stairs with the peeling banister, Stewart looked through three bedrooms and a bathroom but found the same state of neglect to household cleanliness but little else. There was a distinct lack of photos in the house except for two pictures of different women. One was in the main bedroom and sat in pride of place on the dressing table. Maybe this was Green's wife. They would have to ask the neighbours.

The other photograph was hanging on the wall in the second bedroom. Stewart studied it as Ross joined her and he took an immediate step backwards as he saw it was surrounded by a large number of magazine cut-outs. Various women from what Stewart would have described as men's magazines—and not the smart lads' mags either—adorned the wall in a need to show off whatever was not normally shown, and it caused a small cough of propriety from Ross. Given his persuasion, this made Stewart almost giggle, but she was deep in thought about the photograph in the middle of the exposed women. A dark haired and dark-skinned woman in maybe her thirties was lying on a beach with a number of large buildings in the background. The sun was clearly shining, and she was dressed in a sarong with a large but loose white t-shirt covering her upper body. The photograph was in no way sexual, an island among the mass of pornography around it and it was this fact that screamed something at Stewart. Why have this? Who was this woman? Not a cheap throwaway thrill but someone who meant something.

The woman was dark skinned but not so dark that you would think her to be from near the equator but rather a lighter shade of brown. Her curled black hair framed a gentle smile and she seemed to be at ease as she posed for this most innocent of photographs.

'Who is that, Ross?' Stewart asked her colleague.

'Don't know.'

'A girlfriend. Not the mother as I think that's her next door. You can see the resemblance to her son. But this is different. Maybe a girlfriend? Maybe an adopted sibling? Maybe a desired colleague given the smut that surrounds it?'

'Whoever it is,' said Ross, 'it's someone from at least twenty years ago if not more. Look at the cars, Stewart. Those are from a time; the styles are just not today. I'd say twenty to thirty years ago and that's Spain. In fact . . .' Ross held his hand to his chin and seemed to be drifting back to somewhere in his mind. Stewart did not interrupt him but instead turned to look at the bed of the room which was at such an angle that the sleeper would face this wall.

'Magaluf! That's where it is. The hotel in the background, knew I had passed it. In fact, we ate in there.'

'Who did?'

'John, before he had the accident. That was one of our last holidays. He wanted some sun and we got a cheap deal to Majorca. We got thrown out of a few bars.'

Stewart watched the man's face as it became a wash of delight followed by a sudden hollowness. 'And you are sure that's Majorca, Magaluf.'

173

'Yes, got the photos at home. You don't forget good times like that. But why have a twenty-plus-year-old photo of some random woman among all this sleaze? Doesn't make sense.'

Stewart stepped back to the wall and lifted off one of the sleazier pictures, discovering it was held on with Blu-tac. Taking the picture of the dark-skinned woman, she found it to be hung up with a nail and picture wire.

'The woman was here first, Ross, there's even a light stain behind it.' A rectangle had been formed on the wall where the paint had not been deteriorated by the sunlight. 'Must have been up here a while. But why?'

Stewart walked out of the bedroom and stood between it and the main bedroom which backed onto it. In between was a wall but in the main bedroom that wall stuck out further at the far end of the rooms. There was maybe an extra foot and where the wall then moved back, a clever arrangement of shelves had been constructed that softened the harsh lines.

'Ross, we need to go next door. There's an addition here, I reckon, but if I see next door, we'll know. These houses were all built in a mirror of each other. One side of the semi-detached would be symmetrical to the other. I reckon there's been something placed behind that wall of posing women.

Ross nodded and told Stewart to go and have a look. A minute later she was standing in front of a black door which opened to reveal a smartly dressed gentleman in the latter stages of life. Stewart made her apologies for disturbing him and asked to see his bedroom. The man was surprised but when she said she was investigating something next door he picked up and became incredibly helpful.

'I knew there was something about them. You know Simon had some really dodgy friends, all through his time here. I kept clear of them, as you can imagine but he was up to his neck in it. And as for that boy of his.' Hope reeled; the boy was a full-grown adult probably in his forties. 'Pure filth. You can tell the boxes that are arriving are from those shops. Plain paper. But they dropped one off here one day when he was out. Well, really, no self-respecting woman would pose like that.'

'You opened his mail?' asked Stewart. The man went silent. 'Or was it just ripped, sir?'

'Yes,' the man replied quietly, 'ripped as you say.'

The bedroom showed the same design as its counterpart next door except for one feature, that of the extended wall. Stewart smiled to herself, pushed her glasses back and then winced as her face felt a twinge of pain.

'Are you okay, officer? That's a heck of a bruise on your face.'

'Fine, sir, but thank you. And thanks for your assistance.' The man smiled and escorted Stewart to the door.

Back in the Green residence, Stewart found Ross tapping the expanded wall she had found. His ear was hard to it and Ross was carefully sounding every square inch of the wall.

'That's solid, Stewart. I can't find a cavity but we need forensics. Maybe they can peer into the wall.' Ross peeled away to make the call and Stewart was left standing, her eyes on the opaque plaster before her. Maybe something was in there. It seemed strange having a perfectly normal photograph amongst the porn. Stewart stepped outside to make a call as well.

When she got through to the Newcastle main station, it took her several minutes to track down and then get message to the officers who had taken the younger Mr Green to the mortuary to identify his father's body. The forensic team had arrived by the time the answer to her question was answered.

According to the younger Mr Green, the photograph was one of his father's and had been in the room when the son had moved into that room. When he had tried to move it, his father had gone somewhat crazy and the son decided to simply leave it there as in reality, as he put it, she was a decent bird even if she did have her clothes on. The comment disgusted Stewart but it also gave her a little kick of excitement as she realised they may be onto something.

Ross joined Stewart at the front of the house and took in a deep draught of fresh air. 'They reckon something's in there,' said Ross. 'I've left them to excavate it but they said they would be a while. You want something to eat? Could be a while before we get a natural break like this. Seems we are on a run today, though we did pay the price for it.'

Stewart watched Ross examine her bruised face and then start to raise his hand to her cheek before he stopped. Almost embarrassed, he turned away but she spoke after him. 'It is smarting, and I could do with a bite. One of us should stay though, shouldn't we? Do you mind getting the food? I might frighten them with this face.'

'I didn't mean anything . . .'

Stewart held up a hand and when Ross asked what she wanted, she merely replied, 'Anything.' When he returned with a fish supper, the great battered fish accompanied with chips that was a staple anywhere in the United Kingdom, she wolfed the hot fish into her. It was cod, not haddock, but then she was in England, was she not?

The night was beginning to fall when one of the forensic team called them through to the upstairs room. The younger Mr Green was still helping with enquiries surrounding his father's death and had not returned although he may have had a small fit on seeing his beloved wall of women now in ruins. The forensic team had removed each crass photograph, bagging them for reference and then had broken the wall down slowly. As Stewart entered the room, she saw a plastic sheet hanging over where the magazine images had been.

'Karen Sommes', said an older woman, maybe in her late fifties, but dressed in a white coverall with her hood up and a mask across her face. The woman shook both their hands before turning to the plastic sheet and pulling it back. There before the detectives was a skeletal figure dressed in a jacket and jeans. The skeleton was only half uncovered, and the arms and feet were still encased.

'We still have work to do but I thought you should get a quick look now in case there's anything you can tell from the clothing. Also, we managed to get inside the jacket and to the interior pocket. We found this.' Sommes held up a plastic bag containing a green piece of paper. 'It's a driving licence, old one from before the photographic ones, so it has full details. You are looking at Angel Jones.'

Stewart felt that kick of excitement again—almost guilty—as she stared at the skeleton in the wall. But this was a name, and presumably there would be an address.

'Can one of your team open that package up for us and we'll get a photograph of it? Then I think we'll be leaving you alone for a while as we have an address to investigate, Mrs Sommes.' Ross waited expectantly and Sommes called out for a colleague and they duly allowed Ross to make a quick image on his mobile of the driving licence.

Stewart was standing in a world of her own, thinking. *Angel Jones, bit dramatic. But got in too deep and ended up in the wall.*

Someone to bury the treasure and then leave little clues with the group but none had a full picture of where it was unless they worked or shared together. Except for Angel. So, she was silenced.

'Come on,' said Ross, 'we have an address, let's get cracking.'

The address was on the other side of Newcastle and Ross drove back around the city via the main ring road and out towards South Shields where they located a terrace house. The area was clean but the housing looked cramped and cars lined the road on both sides causing Ross to park some distance from the address.

Stewart knocked on the door and it opened to reveal a man of possibly Arabian origins who looked puzzled to see the white-faced Stewart before him.

'Who are you?' the man asked, his English slightly broken.

Stewart produced her warrant card and introduced Ross and herself and the man turned back to the house calling for someone. Soon a man in his early twenties arrived, the image of his father but with a much more confident tone and impeccable English, albeit with the twang of the Northeast.

'Apologies, but my father does not have great English and he gets scared that he might say the wrong thing if speaking to the police. How can I help you?'

'Well, sir, we are looking for the home of a Miss Angel Jones. We have her driving licence and it indicates this address. Do you know Miss Jones?'

The man shook his head. 'But wait a minute and I'll ask my father.' The man returned again shaking his head. Stewart stopped herself from swearing in disgust at their dead end but Ross stepped forward.

'Who did you purchase the house from?'

The man disappeared and brought back his father. 'I wasn't

born but my father says it was from a white man in his twenties, Mr Davidson.'

'And how long ago?' asked Ross.

'Twenty-five years.'

'Did you get a forwarding address for him at all?' Stewart watched the older man shake his head before there was a commotion in the background. There was chatter from a woman she could not see and then the older man shouted something back. 'Is that your mother?' asked Stewart. The young man nodded. 'Can you ask her please if she remembers the man you bought the house from? See if she has any recollection.'

The woman remained out of sight but answered questions from her son in a brief but quickly spoken exchange. 'She says she remembers him and his woman. They were not married which was a shock to her, as my mother had only just arrived in the country from home.'

'Does she remember the moving address? Anything that could give us a clue about where they went to?'

There was more chatter and then Stewart could hear the woman disappear into the depths of the house before coming back in an excited fashion. A hand passed something to the son, and he held it up for Stewart. On the paper was an address for Carl Davidson.

Taking her notebook, Stewart made a copy of the address and then began to thank the family for their help, but she noted the younger son was looking over her shoulder. Glancing round, she saw a blue mini and a woman getting into the car. With the door open, the interior light was on and the tight top and large earrings of the woman were obvious. And then the head turned, and Stewart saw the woman's face. It was Debbie

MacPhail, the woman who had attacked her and killed Simon Green.

'That's MacPhail's girl' shouted Stewart and Ross turned and ran but the car was away up the street at a crazy speed. 'Number plate?'

Ross shook his head. 'She's gone, Stewart. Come on, we'd best get to this address in case she knows it as well.'

Chapter 20

Macleod sat with the various maps before him on his desk but in truth the images were starting to swirl, his eyes becoming blurred, probably from fatigue. Glancing at the clock on the wall, he wondered where Hope had got to. How long can a woman take in the shower? And then he thought of Jane—she could take forever. A smile came to his face. She was not shy about him entering the bathroom when she was in the shower either.

And then he thought of where Jane was. Earlier today she had been busy with Mackintosh, sitting with the woman as they prepped her for the operation. Exploratory, but there was definitely something to remove—they just were unsure of the amount. Cancer seemed to affect so many people, he thought. It would not have been an easy day for Jane and he deeply wanted to be with her because in reality, it was his colleague, no friend, under the knife. But being the woman that she was, Jane had stepped into the breach without complaint or demand.

If Hope was taking her time, then a phone call would not be remiss. And anyway, his eyes were shot through and needed a rest. Picking up his mobile, he pressed the image of Jane's face and spun his seat around so it faced the rear wall. He was not sure why he did this in a room with a closed door, but he felt a deep need for privacy and, for some reason he could not fathom, there was not enough in this office.

'Seoras,' said a quiet voice on the other end, 'you needn't have called, love. Hazel's out from it, asleep and apparently doing okay from what they have told me. But that's not been a lot since I'm not a relative.'

'How are you?' Macleod asked his partner.

'Fine. Tired and sore, and sick of the damn tea here. I was going to wait for Hazel to wake up but the doctor says she'll be unlikely to rise before tomorrow. There's a room near here where he said I could sleep.'

'Why don't you go back to the hotel, love? Surely, you could do with a rest. Have a lie in and see Hazel mid-morning or lunchtime.' Jane went quiet and Macleod could hear her swallowing.

'The doctor said he'd like me here when she wakes. It's breast cancer, Seoras and they have had to remove a large amount of it. She was scared stiff about this, about not looking, well, she said like a woman.' Jane sniffed. 'She's going to need someone. I'll be here.'

'You're a good woman, Jane.'

'Stop it. Tell me that when you see me.' There was a silence and Macleod wondered what was wrong. 'Do you know how much Hazel thinks of you?' asked Jane.

'She's just a colleague, love. We're the oldies in the team so she just migrated to me as I think she doesn't have anyone else.'

'She talks in her sleep, Seoras. I know you don't mess me about, so don't take this as an accusation, but Hazel sees you in a very'—again a brief silence—'primitive way.'

'What do you mean?'

'Man and woman, primitive. Like you see me.'

'I don't see you just like that!' Macleod felt let down.

'I know but you do see me like that. And that's good, Seoras. And I see you like that too. But that's how Hazel sees you. She really is a lonely woman behind the façade of her professionalism. I'm just warning you because she's going to need someone when she goes back north. Just be aware.'

'I will, love. And thank you; can't be easy knowing she feels like that.'

'Like she can pull you away,' laughed Jane, but it was hollow.

'Got to go,' said Macleod. There was a knock on the door. 'I can hear Hope outside.'

'Now that's the one I fear,' said Jane. 'She's got youth, figure, and struggles to find the right man. She could snap you up in an instant.'

Macleod almost spat down the line about how untrue it all was but stopped himself. This was Jane, always making a joke in the darkest moments, anything to keep the chin up. 'Well then, I'd better get ready for a night of wild passion.'

'You're learning, love; take care.'

'And you. I meant it when I said you're some woman.' Another knock.

'Not simply good but *some* woman. I like that.'

'Come in,' shouted Macleod at the door. 'Hope's here, I'm away.'

'Be gentle with her.'

Macleod stopped himself from laughing as he turned around to Hope. Jane's greatest talent was picking him up, keeping him going in rough times, and she'd been at her best in her present situation. She should have been a platoon leader, standing, smiling, encouraging all as they were under fire. She'd be picking up the weaker ones, carrying them on her back, sorting everyone out.

'Sir?'

Macleod snapped back to the present. He was definitely tired if he was drifting off in front of people. 'Hope, I've been looking at these maps and frankly I can't see anything anymore. Spend a while and see if you can see something I'm not.'

'Don't we still need Dusty's Harbour? I thought we couldn't do anything without the reference point.'

'If there are smaller treasure pockets then maybe we could find one from this map. We might find one of these, might find our killers there, searching. A long shot but we need every shot we can get.'

'Yes, sir. And what about you?'

'I'm taking a walk. I won't be more than ten minutes. Can't see the wood for the trees, Hope. I'm also praying Nakamura will find us something from Kisimul, too. I don't know what but maybe they dropped something in the struggle.'

'Well, she should be back soon. She called me about getting dinner later.'

'Is she okay?' asked Macleod. 'It's a big case for her to operate as lead. Clever woman but she doesn't have Mackintosh's experience.'

'Jona's fine. The case work isn't a problem; it was the struggle on the beach that got to her.'

Macleod nodded, got off his seat and offered it to Hope before stepping out of the station and taking a deep breath. The sea air caught his nose and he felt the drizzle. In the darkness, he stared at the occasional streetlight that lit Castlebay into a kind of gloomy fog in the misty spray that the clouds provided. *It's like a Dickensian London in a lot of ways.*

Mackintosh came to mind and he thought of his first meeting with her on the shores at Nigg, when she had some rebuking words for him. And she was right, but he had not seen the warmth for him then which she would keenly display later. When he thought about it, she did have a pride in her appearance and this news would devastate her on that front. Actually, maybe it would be more personal than that. It was hard to know how people would feel when you had not been through such a thing.

Staring from his place by the shore, he looked at Kisimul castle, and saw lights returning in a boat from the island. *Nakamura must be wrapping up*, he thought. There's always a next man up. Or woman. The job goes on no matter what.

Footsteps from behind alerted him before the cry of 'Sir!' Turning, Macleod saw the local constable and ran towards him.

'Vatersay. Just had a call. Someone on the beach digging.'

'Get a car and let's go!'

The pair ran back towards the station and Macleod saw Hope emerging from the station. 'McGrath, get a detail and lock Vatersay off. I don't want anyone coming off that island.'

With that, Macleod jumped into the marked police car and the local officer drove off, switching on his lights.

'No! Keep it dark but go quick. We don't want to warn them the cavalry's coming.'

The car raced out of Castlebay along roads that would be mocked in Inverness for their lack of markings and sheer narrowness. But there was little traffic and as the car crossed the causeway onto Vatersay, Macleod thought about how they would catch this *pirate*. If indeed it was one of his suspects and not simply a tourist or glory hunter. The real culprits were dangerous, and he was not feeling sharp, although the adrenalin was starting to pump and his eyes beginning to focus clearer than they had before.

As the car wove its way across Vatersay taking the one road that swung along the coast, Macleod wondered which beach the suspect was on. They drove up the middle of the stretch of land adjacent to where MacPhail's body had been found but the car continued straight over before driving into the small village of Vatersay itself. There were a number of compact houses but the constable took a hard turn in the village and drove towards the eastern beach, the one opposite to where MacPhail had died. They were heading for the south end of that beach and Macleod leapt from the car as it came to a halt.

Before him, Macleod saw a pier, but to his left stretched out the full length of sand and he saw a figure there with a spade. Calling his local colleague to follow him, Macleod ran towards the figure, his feet fighting to lift from the loose sand at the top of the beach. The tide was high and there was not much room to play with but the man on the beach simply dug as they approached.

'Stop, Police!' yelled Macleod, as he approached. The figure was a man in his younger years and he was wearing a dark raincoat that stretched to his knees. Macleod was only ten feet from him and slowing up when the man unzipped his long raincoat. The darkness made it hard to see what was being taken from the coat, but Macleod saw something long and cylindrical. Maybe it was instinct because he threw himself to one side as a flash of light and a deafening shot ripped into the night. There came a second bang and Macleod knew it had been a shotgun. He heard the cry of his colleague and tried to scramble to his feet. *Get to the man before he can reload.*

186

But the man was off, running hard past Macleod and his prone colleague. Standing, Macleod ran to the constable and saw that he had been shot in the shoulder. Grabbing his mobile, he dialled for Hope and ran after the attacker.

'Officer down, I need ambulance and backup on the beach east side of Vatersay. Vatersay village, end, near the small pier.'

He did not wait for a reply but instead ran as hard as he could, feeling his thighs burning as he worked through the soft sand. Once he reached the road again, he realised the man had made his way to the pier. Racing through the drizzle, Macleod reached the pier's edge and saw the man in a two-person rib with an outboard which he was trying to start. Macleod did not stop at the pier edge but threw himself off it, dropping the few feet into the water and flung his desperate hands onto the side of the rib.

If the boat had been wooden, then he might have had a better grip but instead his hands slid off the side and he descended into the water. Fighting his way back up, he surfaced and grabbed a rope on the side of the rib, lifting himself up from the water. But his suspect stopped pulling the cord of the outboard and instead delivered a punch to Macleod's head which forced his hands to slip and he fell back into the water.

As he struggled to surface, he felt the outboard propeller start and briefly water rushed past with an array of bubbles. And then all was still under the water. Arms stretched out, he tried to float and as he calmed himself, he began to surface. Once Macleod had managed a few gulps of air, he turned himself over and swam for the steps of the pier. Having dragged himself from the water, he sat there. *What was that all about?*

'Sir, are you okay?'

Macleod heard the officer calling him but he only raised

a hand. He was unclear how long he had been sitting there but he was clearly in some sort of shock. His mind thought about hitting the water, about the feeling of immersion and the bubbles passing his face when the boat departed. And then a shiver ran up his spine. The other officer, he had been shot.

'How is . . .?' He could not remember the man's name. He was sure he had heard it, used it. A local man brought up here, he had mentioned it at one point during these last days. It was gone. Macleod began to shiver and then realised that there was no longer an officer talking to him but a paramedic, the green uniform slightly wet from attending to Macleod. A silver blanket was placed around him and he was slowly led back along the pier to the car he had come in. Around him were officers he knew, coastguards in their blue uniforms.

Why out here? It's not right; why did he drag us out here? Macleod tapped the person beside him on the shoulder, but he couldn't form the words and was placed in the back of an ambulance. The journey was a blur, but soon he was sitting in the small hospital that served the isle of Barra and began to feel himself warming up.

'How is he?'

The nurse looked at Macleod quizzically. 'How is who?'

'The police officer who was shot. He shot him with a shotgun, nearly hit me. How is he?'

'He's in the best place, on a helicopter and making his way to the mainland. Last I heard, he was stable. And you're talking, which is good. Can you tell me your name?' The woman before him was dressed in blue scrubs and had long blonde hair that was tied up behind her in a ponytail. Macleod did not know how they indicated ranks of seniority with these practical uniforms as there were no epaulettes but he reckoned she was a senior nurse by how she carried herself, and the fact that she looked like a maturing woman, maybe mid-thirties. It was strange how he always seemed to rank people. Maybe that was the job talking; you made a mental note of someone in a way that you could describe them over the radio in a few simple lines.

'Detective Inspector Macleod, ma'am.'

'And your first name, Inspector?'

'Seoras. I'm from Lewis.' Macleod was unsure where this sudden familiar tone he had learned had come from, but it seemed to please the nurse.

'You look like a Lewis man, Seoras. You're in a bit of shock but otherwise you're okay. We're going to keep you here tonight as we don't know if you've swallowed any water. Do you remember?'

'I don't think so.' Macleod stared at his feet and found himself looking at the design on his shoes. 'Do you do coffee?'

Hope had seen Macleod packaged away in the ambulance and was watching Jona and her team move in with their huge spotlights to start examining the area in the dark. The poor woman seemed to just race from one place to another and they had struggled to meet in the last hours for a pre-arranged yoga session.

Things had got hectic with Macleod's phone call and when she had arrived on scene, there was an officer down and a medical evacuation to deal with as well as organising some boats to try and spot the suspect. But in the dark it was all to no avail and Hope had no idea where he had run to.

Macleod was also in a state of shock and Hope believed it must have been the water that did it for she had never known Seoras to react this way to an attack on him. And the water had so many connotations for him, starting with his wife's suicide and then the rescue at Stornoway on their first case together. He'd be all right, she was sure, but for now he was not functioning like himself.

Hope saw Jona on her mobile phone, not speaking but listening intently. But she had a frustrated face as if no one were speaking. After a few moments, she walked over.

'Hope, can you get your officers back to the community hall. I can't get Gregory to answer his mobile.'

Grabbing a radio, Hope called up for the constable at the hall but there was no reply. She then called the station in Castlebay who responded and said they would send a runner round right away. 'You should expect a call soon, Jona,' she said; 'must be struggling with signal and that.' But something sat uneasy with her. Neither man at the hall had responded. Two minutes later, her mobile rang.

'Sergeant, there's been a break-in. You need to get over here now.'

Giving brief instructions to a nearby constable, Hope jumped in a car and drove briskly back to the village hall. There was an ambulance outside, blue lights flashing in the night and a number of officers standing guard. One nodded at Hope as she walked past him and entered the village hall. Inside, the neatly arranged evidence bags had been strewn about and the place was a sight. In the middle of the room, two paramedics were crouched around someone and one was pushing down on the chest of a prone figure. Across the hall, a man dressed in jeans and a light red jumper was up against the wall, shaking and holding his head in his hands. Beside him a constable was trying to calm him down but the man was having none of it.

'Gregory, ma'am,' said the female constable beside the agitated man. 'He was here when they did that to Simon.'

'Explain.'

'A man and a woman came in here with Simon in the clutch of the man. It seems they knifed him in front of Gregory, screaming for maps, for Gregory to get them or they would knife Simon. After he gave them all the maps he could find, they knifed Simon anyway and then fled.'

'And we're all over on Vatersay, dammit.'

Another pair of ambulance crew arrived and watched them package Simon up and take him out to the awaiting ambulance. Hope stood up and looked around the room while the constable continued to sit with Gregory.

All the maps, all the damn maps, thought Hope. *They have all they need and we're clueless still—still don't know where the treasure is to intercept them. And Seoras is down, right when I need him here. It's all on Stewart or these killers will be gone with everything they came for.*

Chapter 21

Stewart stood in front of another door in a different part of Newcastle. This time they were closer to the city centre and were three floors up. A large African man answered the door and Stewart reckoned he must have been at least six and a half feet tall. Even Ross was dwarfed by him, never mind Stewart with her smaller stature.

'Sir, we are looking for a Carl Davidson with regard to an investigation we are carrying out. Do you know his whereabouts?'

The man looked nervous and simply said nothing.

'It's for his safety, sir.'

'Carl has moved,' came a slow and very deliberate reply. 'And he's taken his addicts with him.'

'Addicts, sir?'

'I bought this flat from him two years ago and then all these junkies turn up trying to score. Been two months since I saw the last of them—wouldn't listen that Carl had moved.'

Stewart pushed her glasses further up her nose and saw the man staring at the side of her face. 'Do you have a new address for him?'

'Sure, but I doubt it's real. Every bloody junkie kept coming back until I persuaded them otherwise. I'll go get it for you.'

With the man gone, Stewart heard a whisper from Ross. 'I'm sure he's very persuasive.' Stewart forced herself not to laugh.

'Here,' said the man returning and Stewart noted the address down in her notebook. *Inverie*.

When they had returned to the car, Stewart noted the time and saw that midnight had arrived. 'Well, we can check this in the morning, Ross, time to get some sleep. Been a bit of a rough day.'

Ross took the hint and started the car, ready to drive to their hotel. But before he could press the accelerator, his mobile rang. 'Ross here. Yeah, put it on speaker, Stewart's here with me, McGrath.'

Together, Stewart and Ross listened in horror at the tale Hope laid out for them, of how Macleod was now in the hospital and two constables were seriously injured and possibly fighting for their lives.

'And they have everything they need if they get Dudley. For all we know, they could be there already. What do you have?'

'We're chasing a lead for the woman who buried the treasure. As you know she was buried in the wall of Simon Green's house, but her partner is still alive. It's tenuous but it's all we have. We're going to Inverie in the morning to find him, or at least the next in his long list of house moves.'

'No, you're driving tonight.' Hope was insistent.

'Do you know where Inverie is? We haven't had a chance to look up the Satnav.'

'Knoydart, up from Mallaig.'

'Seriously,' Ross burst in. 'But you can't get to Knoydart without a two-day hike or a boat.'

'Well, get on it, Ross. We're up to our eyes over here. And don't hang about.'

193

The mobile went silent and Ross started the engine. 'Hotel and then Mallaig, and you'll need to get hold of something that can get us over there. In fact, try the helicopters now. There's enough of a body count to justify it.'

Stewart dipped her glasses at him. The comment was crass, but it was also absolutely true. With the amount of blood spilt, the justification to spend to bring the killers to justice was not a hard argument to make. As Ross drove to the hotel, Stewart tried in vain to get a helicopter to fly them to Knoydart.

'They say it's a no go with the weather over the next twenty-four hours. The cloud's too low and then the wind's coming in. Looks like it's going to be a real howler.'

'Right then, bags and we go. We'll have to try for a boat and get there before the wind starts; otherwise, we might struggle to get round at all, and I am not doing a two-day walk in this nonsense.'

Stewart called the Newcastle station to advise them of their plan while Ross drove back to the hotel. They took ten minutes over collecting their bags before starting north, driving the A1 to Edinburgh before cutting across to Glasgow and then out to the west coast. Ross stopped once to pick up some food and drinks at a service station. Sitting in the seat opposite, Stewart had been determined to stay awake as Ross drove, occasionally chatting to her partner to keep him alert but at some point after Glasgow, she had nodded off and did not awake until the city was far behind them.

Before she had fallen asleep, Stewart had been calling several numbers in an attempt to secure a boat for passage to Inverie. Due to the lateness of the hour, she had little luck in actually speaking to anyone, but she had managed to leave several messages and now she was awake, she checked her email to find a reply.

'I've got us a motorboat to take us over, Ross. Are you holding up?'

Ross, blinking his eyes in the dark of the early morning, gave out a yawn. 'Fresh as a daisy. Did you sleep all right?'

Stewart thought this an odd question considering she had been tucked tight in a car seat and not in a comfortable bed, but she nodded anyway. It would be harsh to complain when the man had taken all of the driving. In truth, she had not slept well. Her dreams had been fraught with being punched in the face and the threat of death from a woman dressed like she was working the street. She never actually saw their suspect's face but that fear of being her victim hung throughout her overly active nightmares.

When Mallaig arrived, it was a relief to both and parking the car at the harbour, Ross took some time standing in the early morning cool trying to revive himself. Their boat would be there at nine and Stewart walked the town in search of breakfast returning to the car and finding Ross asleep inside. Moments like this showed the lie in the glamour of police work.

A small but powerful rib arrived at nine o'clock on the dot and having woken Ross for his breakfast, the pair and their transport took the reasonably short trip around the coast to Knoydart and the small village of Inverie. The sun was up but hidden behind a wall of grey cloud and there was a dampness in the air. But the cool and the spray of the sea seemed to wake Stewart up as she sat at the rear of the boat, decked out in her lifejacket. Ross, however, was sitting with his back up against a seat with his head hanging low. His snores made the pilot laugh but the rest was brief as the boat rounded into the loch and came to the pier at Inverie.

With her mobile in hand, and a saved picture of a map showing the location of Carl Davidson's latest abode, Stewart led the way, Ross silent in her wake and she wondered if he was actually sleep walking. Inverie was becoming alive but being winter and given its remoteness, there were few people about and Stewart only managed a nod to the occasional dog walker.

Carl Davidson's house had a small, green hedge running around it and was a small bungalow painted white, although the sharp edge of the colour had faded. Stewart passed through a green-painted gate and knocked on the front door. No answer was forthcoming so she tried again and Ross, in an automatic response, strolled around the outside of the bungalow, peering into any window he could find.

'Knock louder, he's in!' shouted Ross from the rear of the house and Stewart gave the door a battering. There was a commotion inside and then the door swung open to a man in a dressing gown looking startled and then indignant.

'What the hell, love?' The man was short, no taller than Stewart, and he stared at her. 'Wow, that must have been a heck of a thump. Did someone hit you?'

'DC Stewart and this,' said Stewart as Ross returned from the rear of the house, 'is DC Ross. Are you Carl Davidson?'

'Yes, that's me. What have I done?'

'Nothing as far as I'm aware but can we come inside. We need to talk to you about Angel Jones.'

The man started for a moment and then pushed the door open wide. 'That's a name I haven't had spoken to me in a long while. Lovely Angel. Mad, reckless, and lovely Angel. Through to the lounge, please, I have a guest in the house, and

196

I need to tell her we have company. Make sure she's decent.'

The man disappeared leaving the officers to wander into his front room which housed a sofa and a television before a stove. Last night's fire was still burning—barely—but the room was warm and cosy. Stewart saw the remnants of two glasses of wine and a few bottles lolling about the floor. Last night must have been good, she thought, and then watched Ross lift a bra off the sofa before sitting down.

Carl Davidson appeared back through offering a coffee and Ross answered in the affirmative before Stewart could say anything else. As Davidson disappeared, presumably into the kitchen, a woman in her fifties came through dressed in a silk dressing gown. She was not overweight but was a large build of woman, standing almost six feet tall, and the gown only went down to her thigh, revealing powerful, muscular legs. If Stewart had guessed who last night's lover had been, she would have missed the target completely.

'Hi,' said the woman in a husky voice before extending a hand. 'Liz Duran, pleased to meet you. Carl never said he was expecting anyone.'

'We're police, ma'am. I'm DC Stewart and this is DC Ross. We're just requiring Mr Davidson's help in a matter. Hopefully, we can shortly leave you in peace.'

Liz smiled and sat down next to Stewart, dwarfing the constable and she saw Ross almost laugh at the discrepancy in size. Sitting in silence, Stewart couldn't help noticing the enormous thighs on the woman and they reminded her of a fight she had taken at her mixed martial arts group with a woman who felt twice her size. But Stewart had won that battle. Nobody knew the tiger she was underneath. And then something reminded her of watching Debbie MacPhail slit that man's throat. Where was the tiger that time?

Carl Davidson returned with a tray of coffee and toast, running between everyone and making sure all were supplied with breakfast essentials. Stewart saw Ross hungrily attack the offering and she decided that questioning duties were remaining firmly with her.

'Mr Davidson, we're investigating circumstances involving a number of deaths, including that of Angel Jones. We'd like to know what you remember about her, including the last time you saw her and who she was acquainted with.'

Carl drunk a large draught from his coffee before settling into an armchair. Tossing back his mousey hair, he seemed to be looking into the past and pulling his thoughts together. 'Lovely Angel. Like I said, no one's said her name to me in a long while but I've never forgotten her. We were friends from school, but she was always different. Angel wanted adventure and we travelled to far-flung countries on a budget. We got arrested in Vietnam, had to run from thugs in Bangkok, and nearly died in the Australian desert. And all before we were twenty-five.'

'But you were living in Newcastle the last time you were together?' asked Stewart.

'Yes, Angel was a proper Geordie, had that gorgeous accent they have, totally unintelligible like, but God, did I love it. It was funny because she had gone away not long before she disappeared.' The man paused. 'You just said she was dead.'

'Yes, sir.'

'How?'

'Murdered, we believe, sir.'

'When?'

'Twenty to twenty-five years ago, something like that.'

'But she left . . .' he counted for a moment, 'twenty-four years ago. Out one day and never came back. I thought she had just left. I wanted to settle down and she just wanted to wander.'

The man's coffee began to shake, and Liz Duran got up and came over to him, taking his hand. The man went quiet before suddenly standing up and disappearing out of the room. Liz followed and they returned a minute later but Davidson had a large album of photographs in his hand. The front of the volume simply said Angel.

Opening the album, Davidson set it down on a coffee table allowing Stewart and Ross to view it. The first page contained a large photograph of an Asian woman who looked full of life and fun. She was dressed in an open shirt with a bikini top underneath and a pair of denim shorts. The weather was spectacular, and Davidson was at her side, bare chested in shorts.

'That's Vietnam. Amazing days,' said Davidson.

Stewart glanced through the album and Davidson's fondness and love of the woman shone through. Beside him, Liz continued to hold his hand and showed no jealousy.

'So, what happened before she left? Did you have a row?'

'No. But she had started going off on her own, and the last time was somewhere on the west coast of Scotland. She never said where and I had started a job which involved a lot of training and learning so I didn't even think about it. Then she came back from Scotland in a strange mood but we made love that night. I remember it well, one of those special moments you recall, and then she left the next morning, not in anger, just off to another normal day. And she never came back.'

'And you never reported her missing?' asked Ross.

'She wasn't missing,' said Davidson, 'not to me. I thought she had just gone off to the rest of her life, travelling and that. She was very free spirited, we had no ties, everything was just in the moment. There are not many people like that, and I loved her for it. But you have to accept the other side of that.'

'Which is?' asked Stewart.

'They just go when and wherever they want. Everything was a wonder to her but nothing was precious enough to hold on to.' Again, he paused. 'It was two days before my birthday as well. But she left me a gift. It was in her wardrobe along with the clothes she didn't want. Strange thing too, a map of Scotland's west coast, her last trip before she left me.'

Stewart nearly jumped from the seat. 'Where is that map?'

'Easy, it's just a map.'

'No, it's not,' shouted Stewart and Ross rose from his seat.

'Easy, Stewart, I'm sure Mr Davidson will fetch the map directly, won't you, sir?'

'Of course, but I really don't see what's so special about . . .'

'Just get them the map, dear,' said Liz, stroking Davidson's forearm.

Stewart cast an excited look at Ross, but he sent a calm down signal in the form of a simple yet subtle wave of his right hand. Feeling a pounding in her heart, Stewart stood and paced the room for what seemed an age until Davidson returned. When he did, he was carrying a framed map which indeed showed the west coast of Scotland, including the Inner and Outer Hebrides. Various points were marked on the map but none had any names. Looking at the legend, Stewart saw one name only, 'Dusty's Harbour'—but every mark on the map was labelled as such.

'Dammit, how are we meant to work that out?' asked a

despondent Stewart. Ross stood up and approached the map, carefully lifting off the front frame. He then removed the map and turned it over to see a grid on the other side. It had some numbers in it but also had letters on the side. Ross studied it for a moment and then took his mobile and photographed the map front and back.

'We need to crack it,' said Stewart but Ross held up a hand.

'Not the Royal we, we the force, Kirsten.' The use of her first name felt like a rebuke but Ross was still smiling as he said it. For so long he had let her lead in this case but now as the moment of truth got closer, she realised he was stepping in to make sure her inexperience and excitement did not defeat her. 'There's no signal,' said Ross. 'Mr Davidson. Would you by chance have a computer and an internet connection? My boss needs to see this right away.'

Chapter 22

Macleod exited the cottage hospital that served the community on Barra and stepped into the awaiting police car. In his hand, he clutched the printed map and grid sent through from Ross and Stewart. Prior to being discharged, he had taken a moment to study it but was at a loss. He had given orders for it to go to Glasgow and Inverness, to those who studied cryptography but so far there had been nothing returned.

Teams had been sent to scour Barra, checking beaches and coves for anyone digging. Moving further afield to other islands would require such a ridiculous amount of manpower and resources that Macleod figured time was better spent where he knew the MacPhails currently were. They had the maps though and could make a bid for the final treasure at any point. *Loot, Seoras, it's loot, ill-gotten gains,* he reminded himself.

There was a rage inside that had not subsided at last night's deception which had left the forensic hall undermanned and contributed to the stealing of the maps they had obtained, one of which would have prevented the MacPhails from completing the task.

As the car pulled up to the station, Macleod stepped out past reporters, ignoring every request for a comment. There would be enough comments demanded by his superior if they did not solve this riddle in his hands and get the MacPhails behind bars. Inside the station, there was hush as he entered, and Macleod realised why when he saw Hope and Jona Nakamura waiting for him in his office.

'Morning, sir,' said Hope as he entered but Macleod slammed the door.

'How did we manage that fiasco last night? Tell me that.' Macleod stood by his seat, eyes fixed on the pair before him. Noting Hope's angry face, he turned to Jona. 'Surely maps like these should have been locked up.'

'We were working, sir, and then got the call. Some of my team are medically trained to a higher standard than your officers, so we hurried to the beach. Lives were on the line.'

'But we are police officers, we expect that. And you are a forensic officer; you know how damn hard we work to get this evidence—you understood the importance of it.'

'With respect, sir,' said Hope, 'we have not stopped on this case. We are all undermanned and running on empty and this tirade is getting us nowhere. I have the teams out looking but the key is breaking that cipher.'

'I have some experience in that field if you want me to look at it. There's also Ansty; he has a background in it too. We might get on quicker than the mainland. They have other items . . .'

'This is their priority,' seethed Macleod. 'But why not, Miss Nakamura? Just make sure the other forensic tasks are completed.'

Jona Nakamura nodded and stood up, turning for the door. 'And Miss Nakamura, get me a solution; see if we can stop this bolting horse before we lose the case. Otherwise there will be egg on all of us and hell to pay. Do you understand me?'

Jona narrowed her eyes but gave a simple, single nod, almost bowing as she left. Hope stood and shut the door behind her before turning to Macleod hands on hips.

'What the hell, Seoras! That poor girl has been dropped in it up to her neck and you give her the damn riot act over something that was not her fault. We didn't protect the hall. I dropped the ball and you went racing off in a flash not waiting for back-up to people who are known murderers, and rough bastards at that. You can get off your high and mighty act and come down to earth with us mere mortals, sir!'

The last words were almost shouted, and Macleod's face went red. 'Don't ever talk to your commanding officer like that,' he said in an even tone, but he was shaking. 'I needed you here, McGrath, needed you to cover all the bases and you didn't. You missed it, the one important thing not to overlook. We thought we were chasing them, but they played a trap and we were so dumb we couldn't even spot the red herring from a mile away. That's our job, you and me, see the big picture, cover off bases. Jona missed procedure and yes, I get she's tired; we're all bloody tired.' His voice began to waver as it became more emotional.

'But some of us are carrying more,' he continued. 'That's why you needed to be here and not chasing leads. Don't you get it, Stewart's there because she can't do this job! She can't do my job.'

Hope watched him collapse in his chair. 'What's happening, sir?'

Macleod sat forward, rubbed his eyes with a thumb and forefinger and then looked directly at Hope. 'Only between you and me.' When she nodded, he continued. 'Hazel got a diagnosis—they suspected cancer. She called me from the hospital. She was in tears, Hope, must have been five hours if not more on and off talking. Jane's with her in Glasgow but she wanted me. She's a mess. They had to operate. Breast cancer, Hope. They got it but she's not the same woman, her words, not mine. She feels like she's lost a part of her, and she has.'

'Is she stable?'

'I don't know, do I?' spat Macleod. 'Jane's making sure she gets the counsellors and the medical staff today but last night it was me. I'm not cut out for that sort of intimate conversation, especially when it's so bleak, so close to the bone.'

'But why you, sir?' asked Hope.

'Because she doesn't have anyone else. That's what's up, so go and get me these scum before we lose them.'

Hope stared at her boss and swore he was almost crying. The angry commander who had rollicked Jona was gone and she saw how weak he was facing something that was clearly more personal to him than she would have thought.

'She's lucky to have you.'

'Don't, Sergeant—just get me these murderers.'

Hope turned and exited the room quietly. She would check how the searches were going, how they were covering the beaches, making sure it was to order. But then she would see Jona, because if they could crack the cipher, they might even get ahead of things.

The night had closed in and Hope stood watching Jona from a distance. For three hours the woman had been pouring over the cipher, occasionally swearing and waving away all onlookers. Hope had brought coffee in between talking to the search co-ordinator about how things had proceeded.

Today they had searched the island—helicopters, people on foot, dogs, and even a RNLI lifeboat assisting before it had to disappear to a fishing boat that was taking on water. But they found nothing and with darkness falling, the search was being called off. Hope felt an emptiness at that because she knew this was the time the MacPhails would move, out of sight, wherever the treasure was located. It felt like she was describing a movie at times, all slightly surreal that someone had been sent to hide treasure, or ill-gotten gains. But that was what pirate treasure was, loot, stolen items whether by force or by subterfuge.

Macleod's mood had worsened throughout the day and Hope could see the pressure on his shoulders. She had taken most of the press briefings and had talked at length with Ross and Stewart about Carl Davidson and Angel Jones. The brutality of having someone killed and stowed in a wall in your house because she knew where the loot was struck Hope as something the movies would have made out to be business. But when the girl had simply completed a job as requested, to kill her seemed so cold. But Debbie MacPhail had been cold to a man who was at least interested in her body if not more of her. Stewart had been full of detail about that incident. Indeed, Hope was worried that it had scarred her colleague.

Hope started to walk towards Jona and saw a hand being raised.

'Go away, if I have it, I'll tell you.'

'Are you close?' asked Hope. 'All we need is Dusty's Harbour. Or rather the right Dusty's Harbour.' The map obtained by Stewart had shown numerous locations all coded the same, but you needed all the maps and Dusty's Harbour to actually locate the real haul of loot. Every map had a smaller deposit, identifiable from that map but the larger haul would have to be sought together, in life or death.

'I don't mean to be rude, Hope,' said Jona Nakamura, her colleague's name said in a whisper, 'but you're in the way. So, piss off and find something to do. When I have it, I will come to you directly. I have a mobile; you have one too. So, piss off, girlfriend.'

Hope smiled and turned away. She had never had anyone call her friend. Lover, colleague, even wench, though he did not last long, but never friend. Maybe that was what she needed for a while—just a friend. Being a lover with Allinson was not working out so why not a friend to have fun with. Nothing sexual involved. It sounded good.

'Hope.'

She spun on hearing Jona's voice. 'Yes?'

'Think I've cracked it, I really do. In fact, I cracked it twenty minutes ago, but I was checking as the words derived from the cipher made no sense. I thought I was wrong but I'm not. I think it's another language.'

Hope started walking over briskly. 'What language?'

'I don't know. I really don't. I wondered why there were only eighteen potential letters and thought they had just condensed the English, leaving out letters they didn't need. But it made no sense. I believe the cipher is correct, just transcribing to another language.'

'Let me see.' Hope brushed in front of Jona and stared at the letters before her. There were eighteen in the cipher. But there was no *J* or *Z*. Neither was there a *K* or a *Q*. And there was a load missing from the end of the alphabet, no *V, W, X* or *Y*. 'Get Macleod, now! Go Jona, get him immediately.'

Hope grabbed the maps from beside Jona's position as the

forensic officer ran from the room for the station. Unfurling all the maps, Hope placed holders on each edge and studied them hard. Then she took the copy of the map Ross had found in Inverie and looked at the places before her. The words produced by the cipher ended with *Eileanan Iasgaich*. Hope grabbed Jona's computer and then typed into the mapping system on it and waited. There were close matches but only one came up as a whole name. It was a small island close to Lochboisdale on South Uist.

But that was where Hope was lost. There were words before the place name but none made any sense to her. She felt herself jumping from foot to foot. This was it; they were so close.

Macleod came charging through the door nearly knocking it off its hinges. 'Where is it? What have you got?'

'Jona broke the cipher, sir but it's in Gaelic, Scot's Gaelic, I think. It says Eileanan Iasgaich which the mapping system says is an island near Lochboisdale, but I can't read the other words.'

Macleod slammed his hands on the desk and looked at where Hope's finger was pointing. 'Centre of the cross, it says *right in the centre of the cross.* Pretty crassly too. Like a machine translated it. *Ceart ann am meadhan na croise.*'

'What cross?' asked Hope. 'Is there like a famous cross on that island?'

'Not as far as I know, but then I've never been on that island. It is the south of the Hebrides. It's catholic down here, not Presbyterian like Lewis, so it is possible.'

Hope punched the words *cross* and *Eileanan Iasgaich into the Google and awaited the result.* 'There's nothing in here other than a reference to the islands, an archipelago apparently. But no cross.'

Jona was looking over her shoulder where the image of the archipelago was still on the screen beside the search result. 'There,' said Jona, 'right there is your cross. It's the water between the west side of the islands. So, put the instructions on top of that found in the other maps.' She held firm as Hope tried to muscle in but Jona was having none of it. Macleod looked on in anticipation as the woman took out an OS map and began drawing on grids and lines of distance from the centre of the cross. He could see the water between the small islands, could see the cross shape, upside down and slightly squint to the left but was rapidly losing what Jona was doing beyond that. There was a criss-cross and stepping about as she followed the instructions from each map but then she marked a spot with a pencil and simply ringed it.

'That small jut of land west of Eolaigearraidh, at the top of Barra. That's your point, detectives. That's your treasure.' With a quick cross of the pencil, she indicated the spot further and announced, 'X marks the spot.'

Chapter 23

'Bring the map, Miss Nakamura. McGrath, get the car; I'll make the call.'

Hope saw Macleod race out the front door, still wearing his long coat. Outside, she could hear rain and it was starting to hammer down. Jona was folding up her map and reaching for a short waterproof coat as Hope grabbed her own leather jacket. She could have done with her long overcoat on a night like this but there was no time to lose.

Outside, Macleod grabbed the officer on guard duty for the hall and furnished him with the details of the situation and instructed him to get to the station and send backup to the recently discovered treasure site. Inside of a minute, the information was passed and Macleod turned to see a car with Hope at the wheel. Behind them, Jona exited the community hall and turned to lock up.

'Leave that,' said Macleod.

'But you said . . .'

'I know, Miss Nakamura, but we need to go. This is it, we miss them here, we probably miss them for good. Get in.'

Jona flung open the rear door and climbed in as Macleod took his seat at the front. As the doors closed, Hope opened up the accelerator and the car sped off through Castlebay and out towards the east side of the island. The roads out of the village were single track and with the driving rain and dark night, the conditions were becoming treacherous. Coupled with the trees along the road at Brevaig, Hope had to focus completely on her driving.

Turning to their colleague in the rear of the car, Macleod pointed at the map. 'Find the best place to stop. I take it we can't just park up beside the burial site. So, get us a nearest point for McGrath to park at.'

At Northbay, Hope took the road that broke the circular path of the island and they raced past the beach where the Twin Otter aircraft brought passengers to the island every day when the tide allowed it to land. It couldn't land now as the tide was fully in and with the howling wind, landing would be something of an art form for the brave and foolhardy. The road continued and there was a sudden flash of light which lit up the bay beyond them.

'Have you no long coat with you?' asked Macleod of Hope.

'We were in a rush, sir.'

'Do you want mine?'

'And leave you to freeze? Besides, I can't fight in your coat, and one of us needs to be able to apprehend them.'

Macleod shook his head. 'No, we go silently, find them and await backup. If this is the place, where can they go except the road.'

'The sea, sir, they could always go to the sea.'

'Did you see the bay? It's a high tide and the waves are piling in. They'd be mad.'

'Or desperate.'

The conversation ceased and Hope turned left taking the car through Eoligarry and then Eolaigearraidh. The route had houses smattered along it and the road was tight. At one point, a car came the other way and Hope swerved at a speed she would have thought reckless to avoid it, swinging through a passing place designed for cars to halt and let others through. Macleod said nothing but he could hear the gasp from Jona in the rear of the car.

As they cleared Eolaigearraidh and reached a sharp bend in the road, Jona cried out for Hope to stop. 'Here, this is where we want. I think it's over that way, towards the sea.'

Macleod looked out through the rapid wipers of the car and spotted a vehicle parked well off the road. It was a 4x4 and maybe it was one they had stolen. Either way it was parked somewhere ridiculous for the night they were having.

'Miss Nakamura, you stay here and point the cavalry our way but tell them to make it a silent approach.'

'Are you sure you don't need me?' asked Jona, but her voice was unsure.

'I need you right here. I have all the help I could want with McGrath; she knows how to handle herself in these situations.'

Macleod thought he saw a smile from Hope, but he really wanted Hope, Stewart, and Ross with him at least and maybe another fifty constables if the truth were told. Opening the car door, he fought to get out of the car and felt his trousers becoming wet from the deluge happening around him.

'Can you see all right?' asked Hope, emerging from the driver's side.

'It's not great but it'll have to do,' shouted Macleod over the rain.

He heard a car door shut behind him and Jona Nakamura was pointing a finger past his face into the distance. 'Follow that line and it should bring you round to where the site is. I'll get them to follow you round that way. Don't go up the hill as there's a drop down from up there that you might not make.'

Macleod held his thumb up rather than attempt an answer. Without looking back at his Asian colleague, he set off, pushing into the rain and rapidly increasing wind. Hope joined him and together they fought their way across the rocky terrain that had a thick layer of sodden grass over it. It took at least five minutes to negotiate the initial path to the side of the hill and Macleod could hear the waves crashing against the rocky shore. His stomach tightened as he realised how remote they would be from help. It was not the first time Hope and he had been in this situation, but they would be up against far-younger foes. Maybe it would not bother Hope but for him, the days of youth were far gone and over the horizon. Where was Stewart with her martial arts skills when you needed her?

As they rounded the hill, they saw the land beyond drop suddenly and then end in the sea. Macleod thought he heard a voice and then in the distance he saw a light, bobbing about on the water. After pointing it out to Hope, they made their way forward and then dropped to the ground when they saw a figure in the dark, piling something from the ground into rucksacks. There were spades and possibly a mattock, and a small pile of earth.

They had not dropped down quickly enough, and Macleod saw a man shouting out to the night and a woman coming to him and picking up a rucksack.

'Go,' shouted Macleod to Hope but she was already gone. He picked himself up and ran forward seeing two figures ahead, one carrying two rucksacks and the other carrying one but moving slower. Hope was going for the faster figure, so he ran hard after the slower one, realising that it was not moving fast at all. Within a hundred yards he had caught up and dived at it. Together they crumpled to the ground, the rucksack tumbling to one side and spilling some of its contents. Even in the dark of a wild Hebridean night, he could see the jewels and ornate pieces lying on the grass and it took his breath away.

The figure kicked out at him and he felt a sharp pain in his shoulder, but he reached up and grabbed a thigh, pulling himself on top of the figure. Whilst his strength was not that of yesteryear, he still had the weight of a grown man and he used this by pitching himself on top of what he presumed was a female figure. He heard her let go a sharp exhale and try to reach for him, but he was now fully on top of her and reaching for her arms. Taking one wrist he managed to place a handcuff on it and the woman stopped struggling. Macleod pulled the other arm to him and cuffed a second wrist. They had one, now where was Hope?

Hope's lungs were feeling like they would collapse but the man ahead of her was in full flow. She believed it to be the same man on the beach where Karen Gibbons had died, the one who Jona would never forget, callous and brutal in dispatching his victim. Despite his two rucksacks, the head start he had was enough to keep him ahead as he reached a small tender by the shore. Flinging both bags in, he pulled the cord of a motor and stared back, presumably looking for his sister.

Hope could not see what was behind her, but the man clearly did not like it and he started the tender as Hope got close. With a last-minute sprint and a dive, she managed to grab hold of a rope running around the top of the inflatable and pulled herself up through the water. The man reached down to punch her but as he threw his fist, Hope yanked hard on the rope causing the tender to wobble and change course. The man fell down and Hope was able to pull herself up and onto the tender.

A boot struck her face, but she managed to turn her head and most of the impact slipped past her. But she rolled over like it was a knockout blow. With half an eye open, she watched the man check her movement and think she was out cold, before turning the tender towards the boat. The sea pitched here and there, and she was glad she was lying down now.

It was a short journey to the waiting boat and Hope heard someone calling. The man stood up and threw a rope. As he did, he was standing directly over Hope and she raised her leg suddenly, driving her foot up into his groin. He cried out in pain and she rolled up, driving her shoulder up into him and knocking him over. The tender wobbled and she thought she was going over into the water but something kept it afloat and she dove on top of her foe. Grabbing a pair of handcuffs from her back pocket, she took a wrist and cuffed it to the tender's rope.

'Andy, are you okay? Is that Cheryl with you?'

It was a girl's voice, a teenager perhaps and Hope stood up as the tender came alongside. Maybe in the swirling sea and driving rain the fight looked more like a struggle of fellow crewmates but however the girl was seeing it, Hope was not for hanging around. She turned and reached up from the side of the boat, hauling herself onto it. There was a cry beside her and Hope felt something cut across her arm.

Bikers wear leather jackets for a reason and Hope was glad of hers despite how heavy it felt. The knife had gone through but not deeply and Hope pulled her arm towards herself and looked at her attacker. Stewart had described the teen who had attacked her in detail but Hope could have guessed who this was from the clothes she was wearing. A night like this and the girl was in a pair of denim shorts and a sodden t-shirt that left little to the imagination. And if she was dressed like that . . .? Hope saw the look in the girl's eyes and ducked.

A pair of arms appeared over Hope's head and she elbowed hard behind her, catching the bladder of the person behind her. They stumbled back and Hope turned around to see a strapping young man of at least six foot. She did not dare wait to assess him but instead drove a fist into his face followed by another, and then a third, watching him topple to the ground. But as he fell, Hope found herself being jumped upon from behind and a knife appeared at her throat.

Hope had managed to get an arm up blocking the knife and had grabbed the girl's wrist. She had not looked strong, but the girl was seething like a wild thing and Hope felt her ear being bitten into. Pain rolled across her and Hope felt like she would have to move her hands to assist her ear but that would be her last move, because the knife could then go for her throat. The boat pitched and they stumbled into outside wall of the main cabin.

Her ear was now going numb and Hope swore it had ripped. Bit by bit the girl's stronger position was causing Hope to weaken and Hope knew she had to do something. Again, the boat lurched and they stumbled backwards in their clinch. But the boat then pitched the other way and Hope went with it, half running and then bending down, placing the head of the girl, who was still gripping onto Hope's back at a horizontal angle, before Hope's head. And Hope threw herself into the exterior cabin wall.

The girl's grasp fell apart as her head struck the cabin side and they both collapsed but Hope was ready for it and rolled out from underneath the girl. As the girl tried to get to her feet, Hope punched hard and the girl dropped like a stone. Looking down at bare legs, a sodden white top and buttocks half hanging out of her denim shorts, Hope took a moment for a word of victory. 'Tart!' It was not professional, but it felt good.

She staggered to the side of the boat and looked towards shore where Hope saw Macleod staring out to the boat. He had a thumb raised to the air. Hope looked around her, at the man on the tender, handcuffed and going nowhere, the six-foot giant who was still lying unconscious, and to the girl who had ripped her ear. Hope needed rope to tie them up, a pilot to bring this boat to a harbour somewhere, and someone to look at her ear. A raised hand brought back in front of her showed blood. But otherwise, situation under control. Hope raised her hand, thumb in the air.

This is what Macleod needs me for. Let's see Stewart handle this sort of action. You don't get to shove your glasses up your nose at this!

Chapter 24

Macleod was sitting in the rear seat of the police car as it drove back to the station. He was exhausted due to the all-night work at the scene of the MacPhail's foiled escape. Hope had stayed with him after being brought a change of clothes and in fairness, she had been sharp because he had been lacking something. Inside, he should have been delighted, should have been celebrating but there were other things on his mind.

Ross and Stewart had flown in and arrived at the coast across from Eolaigearraidh that afternoon. Her male colleague had been on good form and as usual was helping to tidy up any loose ends. But Stewart had been distracted behind her smiles and she had asked to see Macleod that evening for a 'chat' about the case. For the last week, Hope had been going on about Stewart not being the one to have gone to the mainland and she was right, except for Macleod's state of mind. Stewart was not ready and he would have preferred Hope with Ross. But if Macleod had not been functioning, then Stewart would not have been able to pick up the loose ends. At least not like Hope could.

At Castlebay, Macleod was delivered to the police station where an array of newshounds awaited. Still, now that the case was solved, all be it for the elusive Dudley, Drummer, or whatever else he was calling himself, the press would be all but gone by tomorrow. And he would not be too far behind them. Stepping out of the car, he actually smiled at the vultures and announced he would be giving a briefing in fifteen minutes. Coffee first but he did not let them know that. No, the smile was lost to a busy expression until he got through the station door.

Wrapping up a case took care and focus but he knew Hope was on top of it. And he was glad she was as his mobile rang. It was Mackintosh's number and he took the call inside the small office. The woman was a mess and Macleod sat and listened for ten minutes before explaining that he really had to go and that they could talk more tonight. He then spoke briefly to Jane, who was with Mackintosh, but had to run for his press briefing. He had barely spoken with Jane, almost always with Mackintosh since the operation, but he knew they needed time as a couple.

Someone handed him a statement before he stepped out the door and Macleod stood on a small wooden platform as the cameras faced him. Reading off the paper as if he had drafted it himself and not simply scanned it thirty seconds before, Macleod held the attention of the news media and many locals behind them. It was for them he felt glad that this hunt was over. Barra had a charm all of its own and he had not had the chance to experience it properly. Staring at Kisimul castle, he vowed to himself to bring Jane back here one day. Good times often flushed away the horrors he saw in the job.

It was six o'clock when the team sat down for dinner together; an idea from Hope but he was happy to embrace it. They had been stretched and had been communicating on the telephone and by email a lot of the time and she said a little camaraderie would do wonders. Jona Nakamura had also joined them and Macleod made a point at dinner of stopping and toasting the young woman who had performed well despite his admonishment of leaving the community hall open. He wondered if the next case would also be with Miss Nakamura.

Stewart was quiet throughout the meal, not even fiddling constantly with her glasses and Macleod felt a worry growing inside. He would meet her at eight and she had asked to meet in her room to keep others at bay. The station would let people see that she had an issue; they may even overhear and she did not want that.

Hope was full of life at the meal, and between Ross and Jona, she found good companions to talk to. When everyone had got up from the table, she sat beside Macleod, but he waved her away. 'I'll see you at nine for a drink,' he had said. 'You deserve one.'

When Macleod knocked on Stewart's door, he felt weary, as if he were about to take on the weight of the world on his shoulders. Well, it was half true. He was taking Stewart's troubles on his shoulders which were already carrying Mackintosh's. At least the pressure of the case had fallen from them.

The door opened and Stewart stood in a pair of black trousers and a white blouse, her hair tied up behind her.

'Sir, thank you for coming to see me. I want to make a few things clear about how I have been feeling.'

'Shall I step inside?' asked Macleod and gently pushed his way in. 'And if it's that serious, Kirsten, drop the sir. What's up? Nothing goes from here to anyone—just tell me what's the matter.'

Stewart turned and walked to her bed, sitting down on it, while Macleod made for a chair. But then he saw her shoulders shaking and sat down directly beside her. He heard a snivel and then saw red eyes as she looked at him. There were tears streaming down her face and she was leaning forward trying to control the juddering that was coursing through her body.

'She would have killed me but for him. She would have simply disposed of me. And then she just . . . slit his throat. I couldn't save him, couldn't stop her. She killed Green, too. Blood everywhere, all over Ross. Standing there, looking at me, hanging all to show for him and then she killed him. I can't do this, sir. I can't. Not that.'

Macleod thought about saying something but instead simply held his colleague as she cried. By procedure, he should, of course, have Hope with him and this should be in a police station, but Kirsten had not wanted that. Holding her tight, all Macleod said was, 'I know' and let the woman sob.

Kirsten was not the first officer to fall apart; he had done so himself and was feeling no anger or any less of her for it. Instead, he had a worry that she might not get over it. The woman was a thinker, someone who delved into people and things with a fine-tooth comb. But there are some parts of people that should not be looked into, at least if you want to keep on the front line of the job.

Before he left her, Macleod talked to Stewart about getting proper help and doing it discreetly. She was worried how it would look but he told her it would help and that he would put Hope in charge of seeing Stewart got the required help. The two needed to bond better.

When he entered the bar at ten o'clock, Macleod saw Hope holding a Mojito amongst several locals and travellers. She

221

pointed to a cup of coffee and he gladly took it up. There were cries of congratulations from several local people and Macleod acknowledged them. They were victims too, having lost one of their own by accident. It was then his mobile rang and he saw Jona Nakamura's number.

'Sir, I've been called out back to the site of last night's activities at Eolaigearraidh. One of the team was surveying the land and saw a patch of land that looked odd. We didn't get to it until later today because of the obvious other work, but there's a body here. It looks like the old man who was in the gang—Drummer, or Dudley, as we now believe him to be called.'

'I thought he had run,' said Macleod. 'How was he killed?'

'Knife across the throat. Bled out by the looks of it and then was buried. I'll need one of you up here but there's no rush.'

'I'll be up there in an hour,' said Macleod. Clearing the call, Macleod nodded to Hope to join him outside and they stepped into a damp night, but the wind had died away and there was a break in the cloud. Before them, they saw Kisimul castle bathed briefly in a tight shaft of moonlight before it moved away as the clouds drifted on.

'That was Miss Nakamura. Dudley is dead, found in a shallow grave close to where we were last night. I'm going up in an hour to do the formalities. But I need a coffee first and then I have a telephone call to make.'

Hope looked at him with concern. 'You've been up all night. Let me do it, or maybe even Ross or Stewart.'

'I'll take Ross with me.' He saw Hope's disenchanted face. 'He can do the bulk of the work. I need an excuse to cut off my call. And you need to go and see Stewart. Kirsten needs help, Hope. The young MacPhail was seconds from killing her and she then saw her saviour killed before her. It isn't dropping from her. I want you to help her out. Full works, whatever's needed but let her direct. Understand?'

'Aye, sir. But she did go to you I take it?'

'She did, Hope, and not you—which is an issue. You both need to get closer and stop this competition. You're both on the team because I need you and you're both damn good officers. So just stop competing. I have enough to do without that. And besides, you're her Sergeant so she should go to you.'

Hope was about to respond and deny any competition, but she stopped short. *Good*, thought Macleod, *she's starting to self-assess*. 'One day, Hope, you'll be in charge, fully in charge so stop thinking about what others think of you and just do the job how you want it done. You're too good to be worrying about what people like me think of you or how we want to deploy you. Just get on with it and own what you're given.'

'Thanks, Seoras.'

'For what?'

'Trusting me.'

'Rather you with Kirsten than me. Trust me, I'm in for a long night. Now go see her.'

Macleod watched Hope walk back to the hotel and he remembered when he had first seen her. Yes, she had been attractive—well, she still was. But he had missed the fire and drive, and the decency of the woman. Maybe he had a problem that way with women. He got Ross in an instant when he had met him. But Mackintosh had taken time to get to know—Jane too, and Stewart. He totally missed that she would struggle with such a personal threat. They did not build you back home to understand women, merely see their place. No wonder it had taken him so long to be free of that.

Macleod pressed the image of Jane's face on his mobile and he heard her answer in a quiet but hopeful voice.

'Hi, Seoras, I'll just get her for you.'

'Jane, hang on. Let her be; she'll have plenty of time to talk to me. First, you. How's it been for you?'

Read on to discover the Patrick Smythe series!

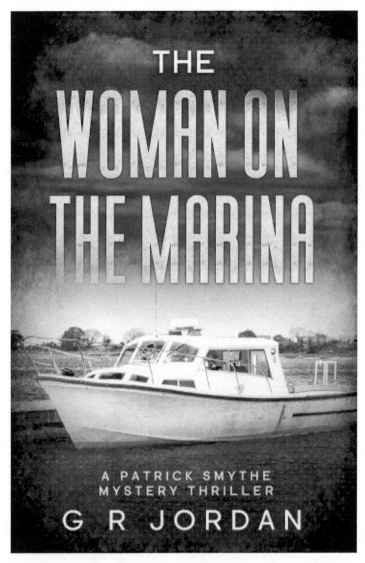

THE

WOMAN ON THE MARINA

A PATRICK SMYTHE
MYSTERY THRILLER

G R JORDAN

Start your Patrick Smythe journey here!

Patrick Smythe is a former Northern Irish policeman who after suffering an amputation after a bomb blast, takes to the sea between the west coast of Scotland and his homeland to ply his trade as a private investigator. Join Paddy as he tries to work to his own ethics while knowing how to bend the rules he once enforced. Working from his beloved motorboat 'Craigantlet', Paddy decides to rescue a drug mule in this short story from the pen of G R Jordan.

Join G R Jordan's monthly newsletter about forthcoming releases and special writings for his tribe of avid readers and then receive your free Patrick Smythe short story.

Go to https://bit.ly/PatrickSmythe for your Patrick Smythe journey to start!

About the Author

GR Jordan is a self-published author who finally decided at forty that in order to have an enjoyable lifestyle, his creative beast within would have to be unleashed. His books mirror that conflict in life where acts of decency contend with self-promotion, goodness stares in horror at evil, and kindness blindsides us when we at our worst. Corrupting our world with his parade of wondrous and horrific characters, he highlights everyday tensions with fresh eyes whilst taking his methodical, intelligent mainstays on a roller-coaster ride of dilemmas, all the while suffering the banter of their provocative sidekicks.

A graduate of Loughborough University where he masqueraded as a chemical engineer but ultimately played American football, Gary had worked at changing the shape of cereal flakes and pulled a pallet truck for a living. Watching vegetables freeze at -40'C was another career highlight and he was also one of the Scottish Highlands "blind" air traffic controllers.

These days he has graduated to answering a telephone to people in trouble before telephoning other people to sort it out.

Having flirted with most places in the UK, he is now based in the Isle of Lewis in Scotland where his free time is spent between raising a young family with his wife, writing, figuring out how to work a loom and caring for a small flock of chickens. Luckily, his writing is influenced by his varied work and life experience as the chickens have not been the poetical inspiration he had hoped for!

You can connect with me on:

 https://grjordan.com

 https://facebook.com/carpetlessleprechaun

Subscribe to my newsletter:

 https://bit.ly/PatrickSmythe

Also by G R Jordan

A Personal Agenda (Highlands & Islands Detective Book 7)
A terrorist kills on the Caledonian Canal. Personal trauma takes Macleod out of the investigation. Can McGrath and the team strip away the killer's masked agenda and prevent another murder?

When terrorist attacks occur in the West of Scotland, Macleod and McGrath work amidst the multitude of agencies to uncover the organisation behind it. But just as Macleod makes a startling revelation, a crisis at home removes him from the team. With the country's agencies chasing down a blind alley, can newly promoted DS McGrath pull her team together and stop one final killing?

There's no wilder face of terror than the one with a personal agenda!

Highlands and Islands Detective Thriller Series

Join stalwart DI Macleod and his burgeoning new female DC McGrath as they look into the darker side of the stunningly scenic and wilder parts of the north of Scotland. From the Black Isle to Lewis, Mull to Harris and across to the small Isles, the Uists and Barra, this mismatched pairing follow murders, thieves and vengeful victims in an effort to restore tranquillity to the remoter parts of the land.

Be part of this tale of a surprise partnership amidst the foulest deeds and darkest souls who stalk this peaceful and most beautiful of lands, and you'll never see the Highlands the same way again.

The Fairy Pools Gathering
A desperate woman fears her husband's sudden change. Men in white perform ceremonies in the dark. Can Paddy unmask the terror that's putting businesses to the sword?

When Patrick Smythe is asked to investigate a woman's plea about a man's mid-life crisis, he sends his young partner to an easy mark. But when a local tourist site becomes the scene for strange meetings and intimidation, Paddy and Susan are drawn into the underworld of the local tourist industry.

"The Fairy Pools Gathering" is the third full Patrick Smythe adventure involving the Ulster native and one-armed investigator with a knack for finding dangerous situations amidst lies and deceit. If you love fast-paced action and an underdog to root for, Patrick Smythe will fly all your kites.

It's all smoke and mirrors until someone gets hurt!

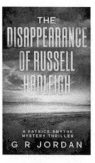 **The Disappearance of Russell Hadleigh (Patrick Smythe Book 1)**
A retired judge fails to meet his golf partner. His wife calls for help while running a fantasy play ring. When Russians start co-opting into a fairly-traded clothing brand, can Paddy untangle the strands before the bodies start littering the golf course?

In his first full novel, Patrick Smythe, the single-armed former policeman, must infiltrate the golfing social scene to discover the fate of his client's husband. Assisted by a young starlet of the greens, Paddy tries to understand just who bears a grudge and who likes to play in the rough, culminating in a high stakes showdown where lives are hanging by the reaction of a moment. If you love pacey action, suspicious motives and devious characters, then Paddy Smythe operates amongst your kind of people.

Love is a matter of taste but money always demands more of its suitor.

Lightning Source UK Ltd.
Milton Keynes UK
UKHW040705291122
413053UK00001B/147